IF SHE FLED

BLAKE PIERCE

Blake Pierce is author of the bestselling RILEY PAGE mystery series, which includes fifteen books (and counting). Blake Pierce is also the author of the MACKENZIE WHITE mystery series, comprising thirteen books (and counting); of the AVERY BLACK mystery series, comprising six books; of the KERI LOCKE mystery series, comprising five books; of the MAKING OF RILEY PAIGE mystery series, comprising four books (and counting); of the KATE WISE mystery series, comprising six books (and counting); of the CHLOE FINE psychological suspense mystery, comprising five books (and counting); and of the JESSE HUNT psychological suspense thriller series, comprising five books (and counting).

ONCE GONE (a Riley Paige Mystery—Book #1), BEFORE HE KILLS (A Mackenzie White Mystery—Book 1), CAUSE TO KILL (An Avery Black Mystery—Book 1), A TRACE OF DEATH (A Keri Locke Mystery—Book 1), and WATCHING (The Making of Riley Paige—Book 1) are each available as a free download on Amazon!

An avid reader and lifelong fan of the mystery and thriller genres, Blake loves to hear from you, so please feel free to visit www. blakepierceauthor.com to learn more and stay in touch.

BOOKS BY BLAKE PIERCE

A JESSIE HUNT PSYCHOLOGICAL SUSPENSE SERIES
THE PERFECT WIFE (Book #1)
THE PERFECT BLOCK (Book #2)
THE PERFECT HOUSE (Book #3)
THE PERFECT SMILE (Book #4)
THE PERFECT LIE (Book #5)

CHLOE FINE PSYCHOLOGICAL SUSPENSE SERIES
NEXT DOOR (Book #1)
A NEIGHBOR'S LIE (Book #2)
CUL DE SAC (Book #3)
SILENT NEIGHBOR (Book #4)
HOMECOMING (Book #5)
TINTED WINDOWS (Book #6)

KATE WISE MYSTERY SERIES
IF SHE KNEW (Book #1)
IF SHE SAW (Book #2)
IF SHE RAN (Book #3)
IF SHE HID (Book #4)
IF SHE FLED (Book #5)
IF SHE FEARED (Book #6)

THE MAKING OF RILEY PAIGE SERIES
WATCHING (Book #1)
WAITING (Book #2)
LURING (Book #3)
TAKING (Book #4)
STALKING (Book #5)

RILEY PAIGE MYSTERY SERIES
ONCE GONE (Book #1)
ONCE TAKEN (Book #2)
ONCE CRAVED (Book #3)
ONCE LURED (Book #4)
ONCE HUNTED (Book #5)
ONCE PINED (Book #6)
ONCE FORSAKEN (Book #7)
ONCE COLD (Book #8)
ONCE STALKED (Book #9)
ONCE LOST (Book #10)
ONCE BURIED (Book #11)
ONCE BOUND (Book #12)
ONCE TRAPPED (Book #13)
ONCE DORMANT (Book #14)
ONCE SHUNNED (Book #15)
ONCE MISSED (Book #16)

MACKENZIE WHITE MYSTERY SERIES
BEFORE HE KILLS (Book #1)
BEFORE HE SEES (Book #2)
BEFORE HE COVETS (Book #3)

BEFORE HE TAKES (Book #4)
BEFORE HE NEEDS (Book #5)
BEFORE HE FEELS (Book #6)
BEFORE HE SINS (Book #7)
BEFORE HE HUNTS (Book #8)
BEFORE HE PREYS (Book #9)
BEFORE HE LONGS (Book #10)
BEFORE HE LAPSES (Book #11)
BEFORE HE ENVIES (Book #12)
BEFORE HE STALKS (Book #13)

AVERY BLACK MYSTERY SERIES
CAUSE TO KILL (Book #1)
CAUSE TO RUN (Book #2)
CAUSE TO HIDE (Book #3)
CAUSE TO FEAR (Book #4)
CAUSE TO SAVE (Book #5)
CAUSE TO DREAD (Book #6)

KERI LOCKE MYSTERY SERIES
A TRACE OF DEATH (Book #1)
A TRACE OF MUDER (Book #2)
A TRACE OF VICE (Book #3)
A TRACE OF CRIME (Book #4)
A TRACE OF HOPE (Book #5)

IF SHE FLED

(A Kate Wise Mystery—Book 5)

BLAKE PIERCE

TABLE OF CONTENTS

Prologue· ·xi
Chapter One· 1
Chapter Two · 10
Chapter Three · 16
Chapter Four · 25
Chapter Five · 32
Chapter Six· 39
Chapter Seven· 45
Chapter Eight · 55
Chapter Nine · 59
Chapter Ten · 63
Chapter Eleven · 69
Chapter Twelve · 77
Chapter Thirteen · 90
Chapter Fourteen · 98
Chapter Fifteen· 108
Chapter Sixteen · 116
Chapter Seventeen · 125
Chapter Eighteen · 130
Chapter Nineteen · 136
Chapter Twenty· 139
Chapter Twenty One · 142
Chapter Twenty Two · 151
Chapter Twenty Three· 155

Chapter Twenty Four · 163
Chapter Twenty Five · 169
Chapter Twenty Six ·174
Chapter Twenty Seven · 181

PROLOGUE

M ost days, Karen Hopkins enjoyed working from home. She stayed busy, which was good because her little web optimization business was only supposed to be a side gig but had somehow become a full-time thing—a full-time thing that was going to help her and Gerald, her husband, retire in two or three years. But there were some days when the clients were so damned stupid that she almost yearned for the years when she'd answered to someone else. The ability to pass troublesome clients off to someone higher up the chain would have benefited her greatly far too often.

She was staring at an email, wondering how she could respond to her client's asinine question with a response that would not make her sound rude. She had one of her classical playlists currently playing on Spotify—but not the kind with multiple strings that drowned out the piano. No, she preferred just the piano. Currently, she was trying to enjoy Erik Satie's *Gymnopedie No. 1.*

The key word was *trying.* She was distracted by the email and the occasional question from the man in the den. The den was separated from her office by a single wall, meaning that whenever the man had a question, he basically had to scream it at her. He was friendly enough but good grief, she was starting to wish she had never called him.

"This is a gorgeous rug you have in here," he said, his voice bellowing through the wall, through Erik Satie, and through her collected thoughts concerning this damned email. "Is it Oriental?"

"I believe so," Karen said, calling over her shoulder. Her back faced the entryway to the hallway and the den beyond, forcing her to have to speak rather loudly.

She tried to keep her voice polite…chipper, even. But it was hard. She was too distracted. This email was an important one. It was a repeat client that looked to be bringing in even more work several months from now, but the people running his business were apparently idiots.

She started typing her response, choosing each word carefully. It was hard to sound professional and reasonable when you were angry and questioning the intelligence of the person you were writing to. She knew this very well, as she felt like she had to endure it several times a month.

She made it four seconds in before the man in the parlor called out again. Karen cringed, wishing she had never called him. The timing was all bad. What the hell had she been thinking? This whole thing could have waited until the weekend, really.

"I see the pictures of your kids on the mantel. How many are there? Three?"

"Yes."

"How old are they now?"

She had to bite her lip to not curse at the man. It was important to keep up appearances, though. Besides, she never knew when she might have to call on him again.

"Oh, they're all grown now—twenty, twenty-three, and twenty-seven."

"A beautiful bunch of kids for sure," he replied. He then went quiet. She heard him moving around in the den, including the occasional bit of low-drone humming. It took Karen a moment to realize that he was humming along to the music from her office, which had transitioned into another piece by Satie. She rolled her eyes, really wishing he would stay quiet. Sure, she had called him over to perform a service but he was already irritating her. Didn't most workmen just come over, work in silence, and then leave happily paid? What was this guy's problem?

"Thank you," she managed to say, really not liking the idea of him looking at pictures of her kids.

She lowered her head and got back to the email. Of course, it was no use. Apparently, her visitor was bent on having a conversation through the wall.

"They live around here?" he asked.

"No," she said. She was rather short and blunt this time, going so far as to turn her head all the way to the right so he could perhaps hear the irritation in her voice. She did not intend to give him the locations of each of her children. God only knew what kind of questions he could make out of that.

"I see," he said.

If she had not been so preoccupied with the email in front of her, she might have recognized an eerie chill in the silence that followed this question. It was a pregnant silence, the type that promises something else to follow.

"You expecting any other visitors today?"

She wasn't sure why, but something about this question sparked fear in her. It was an odd question for a stranger to ask, particularly one she had hired for a service. And had she heard something different in his tone with that question?

Concerned now, she turned away from her laptop. There seemed to be something going on with him. And now she was no longer just irritated by his questions, she was growing scared as well.

"I have a few friends coming over for coffee later," she lied. "Not sure when, though. Most of the time, they usually just swing by whenever they feel like it."

To this, she got no response and that was scarier than anything else. Slowly, Karen rolled her chair back and stood up. She walked to the doorway that connected her office to the den. She peeked inside to see what he was doing.

He was not there. The tools of his trade were still there, but he was nowhere to be seen.

Call the police…

The thought raced through her mind and she knew it was good advice. But she also knew she was prone to overexaggerating. Maybe he had gone back out to his truck or something.

No way, she thought. *Did you hear the door open and close? Besides, he's been chatty from the get-go. He would have told you he was heading back outside...*

She froze, a few steps into the den. "Hey," she said, her voice wavering a bit. "Where'd you go?"

No response.

Something is wrong, that voice in her head screamed. *Call the police now!*

With terror blooming in her gut, Karen slowly backed out of the den. She started to turn back toward her office, where her cell phone sat on her desk.

As she turned, she collided with something hard. She could smell sweat for just a moment but barely had time to register it.

That's when something went around her neck, pulling tight.

Karen Hopkins struggled, fighting against whatever was around her neck. But the harder she fought, the tighter the thing on her neck became. It was rough, cutting and digging in deeper as she struggled. She felt a thin stream of blood trailing down over her chest at the same time she realized she found it difficult to breathe.

She fought regardless, doing what she could to pull the attacker into the office so she could grab her cell phone. She felt more blood running down her neck, nothing major, still just a trickle. The thing around her neck grew even tighter. She slowly sagged as she came within several feet of her desk. As she did, all her eyes could see was the laptop screen in front of her. That white screen, with an incomplete email that she would never send.

She watched the cursor blinking insistently, waiting for her next word.

But it would never come.

CHAPTER ONE

One of the many things that surprised Kate Wise in this, her fifty-fifth year of life (with the fifty-sixth just a few weeks away), was how getting ready for a date never failed to make her feel like an insecure teenager again. Was her makeup right? Was it too much? Should she start coloring her hair darker to combat the grays that seemed to be slowly winning the battle for her hair? Should she wear a sensible bra that was all about comfort or one that would be easy for Alan to remove when the date came to its end?

It was a nice sort of anxiousness, one that reminded her she had been through this before. When she had been married, she'd felt the same way in getting ready for a date all the way up through the first year. But now with Alan, the first man she had dated since Michael died, she had been forced to learn how to date all over again.

It was getting easier quite fast with Alan. They were both in their mid-fifties, so there was a sense of urgency to each date—an unspoken knowledge that if this relationship was going to come to something other than dating, they needed to fully invest in it. So far, through a few obstacles here and there, they had done exactly that. And to this point, it had been pretty incredible.

Tonight's date was to be dinner, a movie, and then back to her place, where they'd spend the night together. That was another thing their age allowed them to do in dating: to skip the will-we-won't-we when it came to the bedroom. The answer for the last few months had been an unequivocal yes—a yes that carried over after nearly every date (something else that surprised Kate about dating at the age of fifty-five).

As she applied her lipstick—just a bit, like she knew Alan liked— a knock at her front door startled her. She checked her watch and saw that it was only 6:35, a full twenty-five minutes earlier than she had been expecting Alan.

She smiled, assuming he had come by early. Maybe he wanted to swap the order of the date and go ahead and do the bedroom part first. It would be a pain to get undressed moments after she'd *gotten* dressed, but it would be worth it. With a smile on her face, she left her bedroom, walked through the house, and answered the door.

When she saw that it was Melissa on the other side, she went through several emotions quite quickly: surprise, disappointment, and then worry. Melissa was carrying the car seat in her right hand as little Michelle stared out. When Michelle's eyes found her grandmother, she beamed and started reaching out, making clutching motions with her little hands.

"Melissa, hi," Kate said. "Come in, come in."

Melissa did as asked, frowning as she looked her mother over. "Crap. Are you going out? A date with Alan?"

"Yeah. He's coming over in about twenty minutes. Why? What's up?"

It was then, as they settled down on the couch, that Kate noticed something seemed to be troubling Melissa. "I was hoping you could watch Michelle tonight."

"Melissa...I'd love to any other time. You know that. But as you can see, I already have plans. Is...is everything okay?"

Melissa shrugged. "I guess. I don't know. Terry has been weird lately. Honestly, he's been weird ever since Michelle's health scare. He's just not there sometimes, you know? It's been worse the last few days, and I don't quite know why."

"So you two need some time together? A date of your own?"

Melissa shook her head, frowning. "No. We just need to have a talk. A very long, serious talk. And there might be yelling. And as distant as he's been lately, he and I both agree that we're never going to yell at each other while there's a child in the house."

"Is he … is he mistreating you?"

"No, nothing like that."

Kate looked down at the car seat, slowly taking Michelle out. "Lissa, you should have called. Given me a heads-up."

"I did. I tried, about an hour ago. But it rang a few times and went to voicemail."

"Ah hell. I left it on silent after I went to the dentist today. I'm so sorry."

"No, *I'm* sorry. I hate to ask you for this favor so last minute when you clearly already have plans. But … I don't know what else to do. I'm sorry if it feels like I'm taking advantage of you, but you're … you're all I have, Mom. But lately, it feels like you're moving on. You have Alan and your sort-of job with the bureau now. I feel like you're forgetting about me … that Michelle and I are more of a nuisance than anything else."

It broke Kate's heart to hear those words. She sat Michelle on her lap, holding her little hands and bouncing her lightly.

"I have not forgotten about you," Kate said. "If anything, I think I've been trying to rediscover myself. Through work, through Alan … through you and Michelle. You've never been a nuisance."

I'm sorry. I shouldn't have come over after you didn't answer your phone. We can do this some other time, maybe a few days from now … does that sound good?"

"No," Kate said. "Tonight. Take tonight."

"But your date …"

"Alan will understand. He's grown pretty fond of Michelle, you know."

"Mom … are you sure?"

"I'm positive."

She leaned over and wrapped Melissa up in a hug. Michelle squirmed in her lap, reaching up with a free hand to clutch her grandma's hair. "I was scared when Michelle was going through all of that hospital mess, too," she said as they embraced. "Maybe Terry just never processed it. Give him a chance to explain. And if he gives you a hard time, remind him that your mother carries a gun."

Melissa laughed as they broke the hug. Michelle laughed too, clapping her chubby little hands together.

"Tell Alan I said I'm sorry," Melissa said.

"I will. And if things get weird tonight, let me know. You're always welcome to stay here if you need a break from it all."

Melissa nodded and kissed Michelle on the head. "You be good for Grandma, okay?"

Michelle had no response to this, as she was currently slapping at one of the buttons on Kate's shirt. Kate watched Melissa leave and could clearly see just how torn she was. It made Kate wonder if things were worse at home than she was letting on.

Once the door was closed, Kate looked down at Michelle and gave her a smile. Michelle happily returned it as she reached up for her grandmother's nose.

"Is Mommy happy at home?" Kate asked. "Are Mommy and Daddy doing okay?"

Michelle grabbed her nose and squeezed, as if reminding her of her duties. Kate grinned and stuck her tongue out, realizing that maybe watching Michelle could be a date in its own right.

When Kate answered the door for Alan fifteen minutes later, he looked both happy and confused. His eyes were alight and sparkling as they usually were when they took in the sight of Kate. He then saw the ten-month-old baby in her arms, causing his eyes to narrow into confusion. He smiled regardless, as Kate had told Melissa the truth less than half an hour ago; Alan loved Michelle almost as much as Kate did.

"I think she's a little young to be serving as a third wheel," Alan said.

"I know. Look, Alan, I'm sorry. But there's been a change of plans…like in the past half an hour. Melissa and Terry are going through a hard time. Terry is being really distant and weird. They have to work through some stuff…"

4

Alan shrugged nonchalantly. "Am I still invited in?"

"Of course."

He kissed them both—first Kate on the lips and then Michelle on the forehead—before stepping inside. Kate's heart warmed toward him at once. First of all, he looked handsome as always. He'd dressed nicely for their date, but not *too* nice. He managed to always dress in a way that made it look like he could fit in at a cocktail patio on the beach or a swanky downtown restaurant.

"You think they'll be okay?" Alan asked.

"I think so. I think Michelle's health scare rocked Terry more than he knew. It's just now starting to catch up with him and I think it might be affecting their marriage."

"That's rough," Alan said. He opened his hands to Michelle and she instantly reached for him. As he snuggled her close and she slapped at his cheek, Alan regarded Kate with what wasn't quite concern, but something close.

"Did she not even call?" he asked.

"She tried and ... *damn*. I still forgot to take it off silent. Went to the dentist for a checkup."

She took her phone out of her purse and switched the ringer back on. She saw at once where Melissa had indeed tried to call her an hour and twenty minutes ago.

"Well, you know, we can have the date here," he said. "We can call up some Thai food and watch a movie. And the ending part of it all could be the same."

Kate nodded and smiled, but her attention was still on her phone. She had missed another call as well. And the number had tried calling twice, having left a message the last time.

It was a call from DC—from Director Duran.

"Kate?"

She blinked and looked away from the phone. She hated that she felt like she had been caught doing something bad.

"You okay?"

"Yeah. It's just ... work called, too. About three hours ago."

"Return the call then," Alan said. He was pretending to dance with Michelle and although he wore a happy face, Kate could sense some irritation lurking beneath. But she also knew that he'd only press her harder to go ahead and make the call if she refused.

"One second," she said, walking into the kitchen and returning Duran's call.

The phone rang only twice before it was answered. Even in something as simple as *"hello,"* Duran sounded pissed.

"Kate, there you are. Where have you been?"

"My phone was on silent. Sorry. Is everything okay?"

"Well, when you didn't answer the last time, I've sort of been scrambling around."

"Over what?"

"There's a case out in Illinois—two murders that seem related but there's no hard link. It's pretty much stumped the local PD, and the field office out of Chicago pointed out that you were familiar with the area…the Fielding case you cracked in 2002. They said they're glad to put their own agents on it, but were asking if you'd rather take it. They're kind of excited about the idea of getting you back out there."

"When?"

"I'd like to get you on a plane tonight. Get you and DeMarco out there nice and early in the morning."

"What are the details?"

"I can send you what I have, but there's still some stuff coming in. Police reports, forensics, all of that. Can I count on you?"

Kate looked back over at Alan, still dancing with Michelle. She was bopping him on the nose and on the mouth while he sang a Bob Dylan song to her. If she took the case, she'd have to call Melissa back and tell her she couldn't keep Michelle. Not tonight. And she'd also have to cancel plans with Alan.

"What happens if I can't?" she asked Duran.

"Then I'm going to pass it over to the field office in Chicago. But I really think you're the perfect match for this. All I need you to do is find some leads and get it rolling. After that, local agents can roll with it."

"Let me think about it?"

"Kate, I need to know now. I have to let the local PD and the Chicago field office know what's going down."

In her heart, she knew what she wanted to do. She wanted to take it. She wanted to take it very badly. And if that made her selfish, then...then so what? There was a huge difference between putting family first and denying herself the opportunities and the chance to live her own life. She knew if she turned this opportunity down just because she had stepped in to watch Michelle for Melissa at the last minute, she'd feel resentful toward them both. It hurt to admit it, but there it was, the honest and raw truth.

"Okay, yes, count me in. Are there flight details yet?"

"DeMarco is taking care of all of that," Duran said. "She'll be contacting you soon."

Kate ended the call, her eyes again traveling over to Alan and Michelle. The strained look on Alan's face told her that he had heard the conversation.

"When are you leaving?" he asked.

"I don't know. DeMarco is in charge of the itinerary. Sometime tonight. Alan...I'm sorry."

He said nothing, looking away as he sat down on the couch with Michelle. "It is what it is," he finally said. "And don't feel too bad...I still have a pretty hot date here."

"Don't be silly, Alan. I'll call Melissa and explain things to her."

"No. If they need the respite, let them have it. As you might know, I am fully capable of watching after this little one."

"Alan, I couldn't possibly ask you to do that!"

"And you never would. Which is why I am volunteering it."

Kate came over to the couch and sat next to him. She rested her head on his shoulder. "Do you know how incredible you are?"

He shrugged. "Do you?"

"What do you mean?" she asked, sensing some resentment in his tone.

7

"I mean, this thing with you and your work. It was supposed to be an every now and then thing, right? And honestly, to be fair, it has been. But when it's on, it's *on*. They want you to drop everything and come running when they call."

"It's part of the job, though."

"A job you retired from two years ago. Did you really miss it that much?"

"Alan... that's not fair."

"Maybe not. I won't pretend to know what kind of lure that job holds over you. But I'm on the same sidelines as Melissa and Michelle. There's only so much more of this I'm going to be able to take."

"If you feel so strongly, I won't take this one. I'll call Duran back and—"

"No. You need to take it. I don't want you taking it out on me or your daughter if you let it pass you by. So, go. Take it. But coming from someone who is rapidly falling more and more in love with you, I feel I should tell you that you need to have some hard conversations when you come back. With me, your daughter, and maybe even yourself."

Kate's first reaction was one of anger and resentment. But maybe he was right. After all, hadn't she realized her decision was borderline selfish just several moments ago? She'd be fifty-six in three weeks. Maybe it *was* time she finally drew up some boundaries in terms of her work. And if it meant that her special little set-up with Duran and the bureau came to an end, so be it.

"Alan... I need you to be honest. If me taking this is going to strain us..."

"It won't. Not this time. But I don't know how much longer it can go on into the future."

She opened her mouth to respond but her phone rang, interrupting her. She checked the display and saw that it was Jo DeMarco, the young woman who had been serving as her partner for the last year, riding along on this little experiment between her and the FBI.

"It's DeMarco," she said. "I need to get travel details."

"It's okay," he said. "You don't have to clear it with me."

What she didn't say but felt deep in her heart was: *Then why do I feel like I have to?*

It was a question she did not feel like wrestling with at the moment. And, as she had been doing when presented with questions like this over the last few months, she turned her attention to work. With a sting of guilt, she answered the call.

"Hey, DeMarco. What's up?"

CHAPTER TWO

Both Kate and DeMarco had managed to grab a bit of sleep on the red-eye flight from DC to Chicago. But in Kate's case, it had been a very broken nap at best. When she stirred awake during descent into Chicago at 6:15, she didn't feel very rested. Her thoughts instantly turned to Melissa, Michelle, and Alan. The guilt slammed into her like a brick as she had watched Chicago appear in the soft light of dawn through the plane window.

She spent that first moment in Chicago hating herself. It got better as she and DeMarco made their way through the airport and to the rental car desk.

Now, as they drove into the small town of Frankfield, Illinois, the guilt was still there but little more than a ghost in her head, rattling chains and creaking floorboards.

DeMarco was behind the wheel, sipping on Starbucks she had picked up in O'Hare. She glanced over at Kate, who was looking out the window, and nudged her.

"Okay, Wise," DeMarco said. "There's a big fat elephant in the room and it *stinks*. What's going on? You look miserable."

"We at the *let's-go-deep* level yet?"

"Weren't we always?"

Kate sat up and sighed. "I was babysitting Michelle when I realized I missed a call from Duran. I had to bail. Worse than that, I left her with Alan because Melissa and her husband are going through some stuff. It's kind of eating me up."

"I'm glad you're here with me," DeMarco said. "But you could have just told him no. You're not under a strict contract or anything, right?"

"Right. But saying no isn't as easy as you'd think. I fear I'm putting too much into this. I think it's how I'm finding my purpose."

"Being a grandmother isn't enough purpose?" DeMarco asked.

"Oh, it is. I just... I don't know."

She trailed off here and DeMarco let her have her silence... for a moment. "So, this case," DeMarco said. "Looks pretty plain, right? You read the files?"

"I did. And it does seem pretty cut and dry. But with no leads or clues or even the slightest suggestion from local law enforcement, it's going to be a challenge."

"So... the latest victim was a fifty-four-year-old woman. At home alone two afternoons ago. No signs of forced entry. Discovered by the husband when he arrived home from work. Looks like it was brutal strangulation that cut deep into her neck."

"And that might be the smoking gun right there," Kate said. "What the hell do you strangle someone with that has the ability to also saw into your neck?"

"Barbed wire?"

"There would have been more blood," Kate commented. "The scene would have been beyond gruesome."

"And the reports say this place was pretty clean."

"So that explains why the local PD is having such problems. But there has to be *some* starting place, right?"

"Well, let's find out," DeMarco said, slowing the car to a crawl and nodding ahead and to the right. "We're here."

There was a single policeman waiting for them when they pulled into the U-shaped driveway. He was sitting in his patrol car, sipping on a cup of coffee. He gave Kate and DeMarco a polite nod when they approached his car. He was dressed in uniform, and the star-shaped badge indicated he was the sheriff. If Kate had to guess, he would not be holding that position for much longer. He was easily pushing sixty; it showed the most in his brow and the almost completely gray sheen on his hair.

"Agents Wise and DeMarco," Kate said, showing him her badge.

"Sheriff Bannerman," the aging policeman said. "Glad you could make it up here. This case has us baffled as hell."

"Care to walk us inside and give us the details?" Kate asked.

"Of course."

Bannerman led them up the wide stairs onto the minimally decorated porch. Inside, the house was equally minimalist, making the already huge house look even larger. The front door opened onto a tiled foyer that gave way to a wide hall and a set of curved stairs leading to the second floor. Bannerman led them down the hallway and to the right. They entered a spacious den, the far wall occupied by a single enormous built-in bookcase. The den itself held a single elegant couch and a piano.

"The victim's office is right through here," Bannerman said, leading them through the den and into an area tiled in the same fashion as the foyer. A simple desk sat against the far wall. To the right, a window looked out onto a keyhole garden. A large vase of cotton plant fragments sat in the corner. It looked simple and was clearly fake, yet it fit the room nicely.

"The body was discovered at her desk, in this very chair," Bannerman said. He was nodding toward a very plain-looking desk chair. But it was the sort of plain that would usually boast a steep price tag. Just looking at it made Kate's back and backside feel comfortable.

"The victim was Karen Hopkins, a local for most of her life, I believe. She was working when she was killed. The email she never finished was still on the screen when her husband discovered the body."

"The reports say there were no signs of forced entry, is that right?" DeMarco asked.

"That's right. In fact, the husband told us all the doors were locked when he got home."

"So the killer locked up before he left," Kate said. "Not unusual. It would be a surefire way to try to throw off any investigation. Still, though ... he had to get in somehow."

"Mrs. Hopkins is the second victim. Five days ago, there was another. A woman of about the same age, killed in her home while her husband was at work. Marjorie Hix."

"You said Karen Hopkins was working when she was killed," Kate said. "Do you know what she did?"

"According to the husband, it wasn't really a job. Just a side hustle to make some extra cash to speed up retirement. Online marketing or something like that."

Kate and DeMarco took a moment to look around the office. DeMarco checked the waste bin by the desk and the few pieces of paper in the small tray at the edge of the desk. Kate scanned the floor for any possible fragments, finding herself once again standing by the vase of fake cotton. Almost instinctively, she reached out and touched the soft head of one of the stalks. Just as she imagined, it was fake but its softness was almost calming. She noted a few broken stalks before returning her attention to the desk.

Bannerman kept a respectful distance, meandering back and forth between the edge of the den and the window, looking out to the garden outside of the office.

Karen noted right away that the office desk was facing the wall. This wasn't too uncommon; as she understood it, it was a great way for people with short attention spans to improve their focus. She also knew it meant she likely never even knew what was coming until it had happened.

Her suspicions automatically turned to the husband. Whoever had killed her had entered the house quietly and made very little noise.

That, or they were already in here and she wasn't suspecting a thing.

Again, all signs pointed to the husband. But that was a dead end because based on everything they knew, the husband had a solid alibi. Sure, she could check up on it but history told her that when someone had alibis pertaining to work, there were seldom any cracks in those alibis.

Before stating such a thing to DeMarco or Bannerman, she stepped into the den. In order to get into the office, one had to pass through the den. The floor was covered in a very nice Oriental rug. The sofa looked like it was rarely used and the piano looked as if it were an antique—the sort that was never played but was nice to look at.

The books on the walls were an assortment of titles, most of which she assumed had never even been opened...just coffee table books to look nice on shelves. Only near the end of the furthest shelf did she see any books that showed signs of wear and tear: some classics, a few thriller paperbacks, and some cookbooks.

She looked for anything odd or out of place but saw nothing. DeMarco stepped into the den as well and gave her a frown and a shrug.

"Thoughts?" Kate asked.

"I think we need to speak with the husband. Even with the rock solid alibi, maybe he can uncover some small nugget of information."

Bannerman stood by the entryway of the den, his arms crossed as he looked at them. "We've questioned him, of course. His alibi is pretty much bulletproof. At least nine people at his work saw him and spoke to him while his wife was being killed. But he's also stated that he's willing to answer as many questions as we have."

"Where is he staying?" Kate asked.

"At his sister's place, about three miles from here."

"Sheriff, do you have a file on the first victim?"

"I do. I can have someone email you a copy of it if you like."

"That would be great."

Bannerman's age brought with it experience. He knew the agents were done in the Hopkins home. Without being told, he turned and headed for the front door with Kate and DeMarco behind him.

As they walked back to their cars, thanking Bannerman for meeting with them, the sun had finally reached its place of permanence in the sky. It was just past eight o'clock and Kate felt as if the case were already on the move.

She hoped that was a good omen.

Of course, when they got into the car and she noticed a few gray storm clouds meandering in, she tried to ignore them.

CHAPTER THREE

Bannerman had called ahead to give the husband a heads-up that the FBI was coming by to speak with him. When Kate and DeMarco arrived at his sister's house ten minutes later, Gerald Hopkins was sitting on the porch with a cup of coffee. As they climbed the stairs to meet him, Kate saw that the man was exhausted. She knew what grief looked like, and no one wore it well. But when exhaustion was part of the equation, it made it so much worse.

"Thank you for agreeing to speak with us, Mr. Hopkins," Kate said.

"Of course. Anything I can do to find who did this."

His voice was haggard and wispy. Kate imagined he had spent a great deal of the last two days crying, sobbing, and perhaps even screaming. And getting very little sleep in between. He gazed into his cup of coffee, his brown eyes looking like they might droop closed at any minute. Kate thought that if he had not been overcome with such horrendous grief, Gerald Hopkins was likely a rather handsome man.

"Is your sister here?" DeMarco asked.

"She is. She's inside, handling the … arrangements." He stopped here, took a deep breath to fight off what Kate assumed was a bout of weeping, and then shuddered a bit. He sipped some coffee and went on. "She's been amazing. Handling it all, fighting for me. Keeping the nosy assholes in this city away."

"We know the police have already questioned you, so we'll keep it brief," Kate said. "If you can, I'd like for you to describe the last week or so you spent with Karen. Could you do that?"

16

He shrugged. "I guess it was like just about any other week. I went to work, she stayed at home. I came home, we did our basic married couple stuff. We had gotten into a routine ... sort of boring. Some couples might call it a rut."

"Anything bad?" Kate asked.

"No. We just ... I don't know. The last few years, ever since the kids were all moved out, we sort of stopped trying. We still loved each other but it was just very plain. Boring, you know?" He sighed here and then shuddered once more. "Ah, shit. The kids. They're all on their way here. Henry, our oldest, should be here in the next hour or so. And then I have to ... have to go through it ..."

He lowered his head and let out a desperate mewling sound that tapered into a hiccup-style weeping. Kate and DeMarco stepped away, giving him his space. It took about two minutes for him to regroup. When he did, he wiped his eyes and looked up apologetically.

"Take your time," Kate said.

"No, it's okay. I just wish I'd been a better husband at the end, you know? I was always around, but never really *there*. I think she was feeling lonely. I actually, I know she was. I just didn't want to put forth any extra effort. Isn't that just miserable of me?"

"Do you know of anyone she might have met with the last few days?" Kate asked. "Any meetings or appointments, anything like that?"

"No clue. Karen sort of ran the house. I don't even know what was going on in my own house ... my own fucking *life* half the time. She did it all. Balanced the checkbooks, made appointments, set the calendars up, planned dinners, planted that damned keyhole garden of hers, kept up with family birthdays and get-togethers. I was pretty much useless."

"Would you allow us to have access to her calendars?" DeMarco asked.

"Anything you need. Anything. Bannerman and his men already have access to our synced calendar. We did everything on our phones. He can get you on there."

17

"Thank you. Mr. Hopkins, we'll leave you for now but please … if you think of anything of interest, could you please contact us or Sheriff Bannerman?"

He nodded, but it was clear that he was only a few moments away from weeping again.

Kate and DeMarco took their leave, heading back to their car. It hadn't been a very productive meeting but it did help to convince Kate that there was no way Gerald DeMarco had killed his wife. You just can't fake grief like that. She'd seen plenty of men try it during the course of her career and it had never come off as authentic. Gerald Hopkins was beside himself with grief and she felt incredibly sorry for him.

"Next stop?" DeMarco asked as she got behind the wheel.

"I'd like to go back to the Hopkins house … maybe talk to the neighbors. He mentioned that keyhole garden, right outside the office window. There was a neighbor just within sight of that window. It's a long shot, but maybe one worth taking."

DeMarco nodded and pulled the car out of the driveway. They drove back toward the Hopkins residence as the first of those storm clouds started to creep in front of the sun.

They started with the neighbor directly to the right of the Hopkins residence. They tried the front door but got no answer. After waiting thirty seconds, Kate knocked again but to the same result.

"You know," Kate said, "after working neighborhoods like this one long enough, you almost expect at least one member of the couple to be home."

She knocked one more time and when no one answered the door, they gave up. They left, crossing across the Hopkinses' yard to venture over to the other neighbor. As they did, Kate peered across the lawn between the two houses. She could just barely see the edge of the house that was visible through Karen Hopkins's office window. She was looking at the back of that neighboring house, the front of it situated along a street that apparently intersected the one the Hopkinses lived on.

As they made their way to the house on the left, Kate noticed the first few droplets of rain coming from the scattered storm clouds overhead. They started for the stairs just as she felt her cell phone buzzing in her pocket. She pulled it out and checked the display. It was Melissa. A small knot of guilt gripped her heart. She was sure her daughter was calling to bemoan the fact that she had left Michelle with Alan last night. And now, a bit farther removed from the decision, Kate felt that Melissa had every right to be pissed.

But it was certainly not a conversation she was ready to have right now, as they climbed the stairs to the neighbor's house. DeMarco knocked this time. The door was answered almost right away by a young-looking woman carrying a child who might have been sixteen or eighteen months old.

"Hello?" the young woman said.

"Hi. We're Agents Wise and DeMarco with the FBI. We're investigating the murder of Karen Hopkins and were hoping to get some information from the neighbors."

"Well, I'm not exactly a neighbor," the young woman said. "But I might as well be. I'm Lily Harbor, a nanny for Barry and Jan Devos."

"Did you know the Hopkins couple well?" DeMarco asked.

"Not really. We were on a first-name basis, but I maybe spoke to them like once or twice a week. And even then, it was just a quick hello as we passed one another."

"Did you get any sense of the kind of people they are?"

"Decent enough from what I could gather." She stopped here as the child in her arms started to tug at her hair. He was starting to get a little fussy. "But again, I didn't know them on a deep level."

"Do the Devos know them well?"

"I suppose. Barry and Gerald would borrow things from one another every now and then. Gas for the lawnmowers, charcoal for the grills, things like that. But I don't think they ever really hung out. They were polite to one another, but not really friends, you know?"

"Do you know of anyone in the area that *did* know them well?" Kate asked.

"Not really. People around here are pretty private. This isn't really the block party kind of neighborhood, you know? But...and I feel bad even saying this...if you want to know anything about practically anyone in the neighborhood, you might want to check with Mrs. Patterson."

"And who might that be?"

"She lives on the next street over. We can see her house from the Devos's patio. I'm pretty sure it would be visible from the Hopkinses' back porch."

"What's the address?"

"I'm not sure. But it's easy enough to find. She's got these scary-looking cat statues everywhere on her porch."

"You think she'd be much help?" DeMarco asked.

"I'd think she'd be your best bet, yeah. I'm not exactly sure how truthful any of her information will be, but you never know..."

"Thanks for your time," Kate said. She gave the little boy a smile, making her miss Michelle. It also reminded her that she very likely had an angry voicemail from her daughter waiting on her phone.

Kate and DeMarco went back to their car. By the time they were in and backing out onto the road, the rain had started to come down a bit harder.

"It sounds like this Mrs. Patterson who lives in a house that is visible from the Devos's patio could very well be the one I saw through Karen Hopkins's office window," Kate said. "All those connected back yards with only fences to break them up...that could be a paradise for a snooping older lady."

"Well," DeMarco said, "let's see what Mrs. Patterson has been up to."

Kate could not help but notice how wide Mrs. Patterson's eyes got when she realized two FBI agents were standing on her porch. It wasn't a look of fear that touched her face, though; it was one of excitement. Kate imagined the older lady was already planning how she'd tell the story to all of her friends.

"I heard all about what happened to Karen, yes I did," Mrs. Patterson said as if it were a badge of honor. "Poor dear . . . she was such a charming and kind woman."

"You knew her then?" Kate asked.

"A bit, yes," Mrs. Patterson said. "But please . . . come in, come in."

She ushered Kate and DeMarco into her house. As they went in, Kate looked back at the several items that had clued them in to the fact that this was indeed the right house. There were eight different statues of cats, ornaments that looked like they had been plucked directly from some weird swap meet or yard sale. A few of them *did* look unnerving, just as Lily Harbor had suggested.

Mrs. Patterson led them into her living room. The TV was on, tuned to *Good Morning America* with the volume quite low. This made Kate assume that Mrs. Patterson was a widow who could not get used to being alone. She'd read somewhere that older people tend to always have a television or stereo on in the house after they lose a spouse, just so the house seems alive and active at all times.

As Kate settled down into a recliner, she looked out of the living room window that sat on the east side of the house. She saw the street and did her best to estimate the layout of the yard and the street. She was pretty sure they were indeed in the house she had spied from Karen Hopkins's office window.

"Mrs. Patterson, clear something up for me, please," Kate said. "When we were in the Hopkins home, I looked out Karen's window and saw a house right across the right edge of their back yard. It was yours, right?"

"Yes, it is," Mrs. Patterson said with a smile.

"You said you know the Hopkinses *a bit*. Could you elaborate?"

"Sure! Karen would ask me questions about her little garden from time to time. She has one right there outside her office window, you know. She didn't grow much in it, just herbs used for cooking: basil, rosemary, some cilantro. I've always had something of

21

a green thumb. Everyone in the neighborhood knows it and they usually come to me for advice. I have my own garden in the back, if you'd like to see it."

"No, thank you," DeMarco said politely. "We're sort of against the clock here. We just need you to tell us what you know about the Hopkinses. Did they seem happy when you saw them together?"

"I suppose. I don't know Gerald all that well. But from time to time, I'd catch them sitting out on their back porch. Fairly recently, I've seen them holding hands out there. It was quite nice to see. Their kids are all grown and moved out, I suppose you know. I liked to imagine they were talking about their retirement plans, making travel plans and whatnot."

"Did you ever suspect they were having issues of any kind?" Kate asked.

"No. I never heard anything or saw anything that would suggest such a thing. As far as I know, they were just a standard couple. But I guess any couple could have potential issues after the kids are out of the house. It's not uncommon, you know."

"Did you see either of them within the past week or so?"

"Yes. I saw Karen out in her little garden, snipping at something. This would have been about four or five days ago. I can't be sure. I turned seventy-four this year and my mind is sort of like soup sometimes."

"Did you speak with her at all?"

"No. But there is something I thought about yesterday... something I didn't necessarily forget about but never really bothered to think twice about. And honestly... I don't even know what day this happened, so..."

"When what happened?" DeMarco asked.

"Well, I'm quite sure it was Tuesday... the day Karen was murdered from what I understand. I'm quite certain I saw someone walking around in their back yard. A man. A man that was *not* Gerald Hopkins."

"Did it appear as if this man was trying to break in?" Kate asked.

"No. He looked like he belonged there, if that makes sense. He was walking around like he had been invited, you know? He was wearing some sort of suit or uniform. There was a little badge or patch right here." She tapped the area above her left breast to indicate where she was talking about.

"Did you get a good look at the patch?"

"No. All I can tell you is that it was mostly white and looked sort of like a star shape. But that could be wrong… my sight is about as good as my memory these days."

"But in terms of communicating with either of the Hopkinses, you say there was nothing over the past week?"

"No. The last time I spoke with Karen was when she came over to ask for my recipe for a pineapple upside down cake. And that's been nearly three weeks ago, I believe."

Kate racked her brain, trying to think of any other avenues Mrs. Patterson may be able to help them open up, but came up with nothing. Besides, they had this man in a uniform to check out, so it was not like they would be leaving empty-handed.

"Mrs. Patterson, thank you so much for your time. If you do happen to think of anything else, feel free to call the local police. They can get a message to us."

"I feel like I do need to ask… but with the FBI involved, can I assume the murder from earlier is connected? It's been what… about a week or so ago? I think her name was Marjorie Hix."

"That's what we're here to find out," Kate said. "Did you happen to know Marjorie Hix?"

"No. I'd never even heard the name, honestly, until one of my friends told me about what had happened."

Kate nodded and headed out of the room. "Again, thank you for your time."

DeMarco joined her and they headed back outside, where the rain was coming down steadily, despite the sun still shining through.

Kate nearly took her phone out to see if Melissa had left a voice message, but decided against it. All it would do would be to give her one more thing to stress out over. And if she didn't learn to separate her personal life from her bureau life, she may as well hand her gun and badge back in now.

She hated herself for it a bit, but she pushed Melissa out of her mind for the moment as they headed back for the car.

In the back of her head, a little ghost voice spoke up, haunting the halls of her mind. *Remember what happened when you pushed her aside earlier in your career? It took a long time to repair that damage. You really want to go through all that again?*

No, she didn't. And perhaps that was why she found herself fighting off tears as DeMarco pulled out of Mrs. Patterson's driveway.

CHAPTER FOUR

Sheriff Bannerman was back at the police station when Kate and DeMarco arrived. He waved them back into his office, Kate noticing a shuffling hitch to his steps as they followed him. He held the door open for both of them and then closed it behind him.

"Any luck?" he asked.

"We spoke to a Mrs. Patterson, the woman who lives in the house that you can see from the window in Karen Hopkins's office," Kate said. "She says she recalls someone in the back yard on the day Karen was killed."

"She says she *thinks* it was that day," DeMarco added.

"Sheriff, can you think of any companies around the area that have a logo that is star-shaped and mostly white in color? The employees may be wearing dark-colored suits."

Bannerman considered this for a minute and then started to nod slowly. He typed something into the laptop on his desk, made a few clicks with the touch pad, and then turned the screen to them. He had typed *Hexco Internet Providers* into a Google search and pulled up the first image.

"There's this," he said. "This is the only one that comes to mind straight away."

Kate and DeMarco both studied the logo closely. It was an almost identical match to what Mrs. Patterson had described. It was indeed in a star shape, only the back arm was stretched and slightly curved. A small trail of lines followed the star, the center one containing the word *Hexco*.

With speed like that of a gunslinger, DeMarco pulled out her phone and instantly started dialing the number beneath the logo. "Let's see if there was a service call of some kind to the Hopkins residence on Tuesday."

She sat down, waiting for the phone to start ringing. As she did, Bannerman turned the laptop back around and closed the lid. In a soft voice, as to not interrupt DeMarco as someone answered the phone, he looked at Kate and asked: "You got any initial thoughts?"

"I think we've got a killer that has a certain type of victim he's targeting. Both Karen Hopkins and Marjorie Hix were in their mid-fifties, at home alone. The assumption is that the killer knew the husbands would not be there. And I also assume he had studied the houses, as there was no sign of forced entry. So ... our killer has a definite type, and he does his homework. Other than that ... I'm at a dead end."

"I can try to add to that," Bannerman said. "There were no signs of struggle, either. So the killer knew how to get into the houses without tripping security and then was also able to strike without the victims knowing. It makes me think the victims invited the killer in. That they *knew* him."

Kate had assumed the same thing but decided to let Bannerman get it all out. She rather enjoyed hearing him speak. His older age made him sound very wise and she greatly appreciated his experience. She usually felt as if working closely with anyone from the local police force could be a hindrance, but she was already starting to like Bannerman.

As she nodded her agreement, DeMarco ended her call. "I got confirmation that Hexco Internet did indeed send a tech out to the Hopkins residence on Tuesday. The woman I spoke with said there had been reports of spotty internet service all over the neighborhood around that time, starting Monday night. There were about a dozen other similar calls for maintenance that day."

"Well, it's a huge jump to make, but being a tech for an internet company during interrupted service would grant pretty easy access into just about any house," Kate said.

"Well, it's not too big of a jump, actually," DeMarco said. "I also asked if there had been any Hexco techs sent to the Hix residence lately. Turns out, there was a request put in by Joseph Hix two weeks ago. And according to their records, the same technician replied to both calls."

"Sounds like a suspect to me," Kate said.

"I agree," Bannerman said. "You should know, though, that Hexco is a relatively new provider around Frankfield. A small company. I'd be surprised if they have more than three or four technicians. It might not be such a huge deal that the same tech was at both addresses."

"Still, I'd like to talk to that tech," Kate said. "Did you get a name?"

"I did. The operator I spoke to has sent out a page for him to call me right away."

"In the meantime, I'd like to visit the Hix residence," Kate said. "I know the reports indicate that the scene was essentially clean, but I'd like to see it for myself."

"I've got the key in the case files," Bannerman said. "You can—"

He was interrupted by the ringing of DeMarco's phone. She answered it right away and when Kate heard her formally introduce herself, Kate knew it was the Hexco tech. Kate listened in, so she already knew the details before DeMarco spoke them out loud.

"We're meeting with him in fifteen minutes," DeMarco said. "He seems very willing to meet, but sounded a little scared, too."

As Kate opened the door, Bannerman got to his feet. "Need anything from me?"

Kate thought about it and then, with a bit of hope in her voice, said: "Maybe just get a room ready for interrogation."

The technician's name was Mike Wallace, a twenty-six-year-old who looked very nervous when Kate and DeMarco met him at the little coffee shop three miles away from the Frankfield PD. He looked back and forth between the agents in a way that reminded Kate of those weird geckos that could move their eyes in such a way as to look in two directions at once.

He had a tablet with him, covered with a scarred leather case. The Hexco logo stood out in embossed trim on the front of it.

"Mike, for now this is just standard procedure and you have absolutely nothing to worry about," Kate said. "At present, it seems that you are just having a bit of bad luck and circumstance."

"What do you mean?"

"Well, in the course of the last two weeks, you have been assigned to homes where two women have been killed. The most recent was this past Tuesday."

"I visited a lot of houses Tuesday. There was a pretty bad service interruption in two different neighborhoods."

"You have your service calls on that tablet, right?" DeMarco asked, nodding to the device he carried.

"Yes, I do."

"Can you pull up the entry for the Hopkins residence on Tuesday?"

"Sure," he said. He tapped a few different places, scrolled a bit, and then scanned the page with his finger. As he did, Kate noted a slight tremor in his hands. He was clearly nervous; the trick was to find out if he was scared because he was hiding something or if he was simply nervous being in the presence of a pair of FBI agents.

"Right here," he said, sliding the tablet over to them. "I arrived at ten forty-two a.m. and was gone at ten forty-six."

"That seems very fast," Kate said. "I don't think I've ever had any sort of utility fixed so fast. What was the nature of the outage?"

"There was a bigger one out closer to Chicago. In order to fix that one, we had to downgrade some service in other places. Frankfield never quite came back up the way it was supposed to. It was an easy fix, though. For all but one of those calls on Tuesday morning, it was just a manual reset at the install boxes at each house."

"And it only took five minutes?" Kate asked.

"Really, each reset only takes about two or three minutes. For each stop, Hexco requires me to start the clock on each visit. Once the timer starts, I have to log the visit and then walk to the box. The reset itself only takes about two minutes. After the reset, I hook a test device up to the box to make sure it's working. That takes about thirty seconds. Then I walk back to the truck, enter in a status report, and log out."

He was fidgeting and still trembling the slightest bit. He seemed to notice this and attempted to stop the tremors in his hands by clasping them together on the tabletop.

"So all of that was done at the Hopkins residence between ten forty-two and ten forty-six?" Kate asked.

"Yes ma'am."

"Did you interact with Karen Hopkins during the visit?"

"No. Hexco sent out a mass text and email notice that techs were being sent out. Whenever that's done and the fix doesn't get billed to the customer, we aren't required to meet with them to get a signature. I doubt she even knew I was there."

It all checked out, but Kate did the math in her head. Four minutes was more than enough time to get into the house and strangle someone. Of course, the fact that his report showed where the reset and test had been conducted and logged in knocked that four minutes down to practically nothing.

"Can you find an entry for the Hix residence two weeks ago?" Kate asked.

"Yeah. You got a first name?"

"Marjorie, or maybe her husband, Joseph," DeMarco said.

Mike went through his routine again and had the results within twenty seconds. Again, he slid the tablet over to them. As they scanned the information, he did his best to explain it.

"Right there…exactly two weeks ago. This was a response to a complaint about the speed of their service. They'd called to get their speed and data upgraded but it never took. It sometimes happens when done remotely, on the phone. I went over there and did it myself."

"According to this, it took about fifteen minutes," Kate said.

"Yeah, the little device I use to test the strength of the signal was giving me a hard time. If you want, I can show you the request I put in to Hexco to get a new one."

"That won't be necessary," Kate said. "I see here that Marjorie Hix signed for the service. Did you go inside her house?"

"Yes ma'am. I needed to check her modem. I recommended they get a new one, because the one they had was a little outdated."

For a third time, Kate noted a nervous trembling in his hands. It was too evident to ignore at this point.

"Was her husband home?" she asked, not letting him see that she was noticing his nervousness.

"I don't think so."

Kate looked over the report one more time. Based on the reports and his story, everything seemed to check out. But it seemed too damned coincidental to her. She eyed Mike for a moment, looking for some crack in his façade, but saw none.

"Thanks very much, Mike," she finally said. "We're done here. I don't want to keep you from your work any longer. Thanks for your help."

"Absolutely," Mike said, taking the tablet back. "I hope you catch the guy."

"Yeah," DeMarco said. "Same here."

The three of them left the coffee shop together, Mike giving an awkward wave as he got behind the wheel of the Hexco service truck.

"He seems to check out," DeMarco said as they got back into the car.

"Yeah, he does. But the coincidence factor…"

"Yeah, it kind of nags at you, doesn't it?"

"Well, that and the fact that he was shaking like a whore in church…"

"Nice metaphor," DeMarco said with a chuckle.

They both watched as Mike pulled out of his parking spot. Neither of them spoke, though Kate found herself reaching for her phone, still wanting to find out if Melissa had left her a message ... and just how upset she was.

Later, she told herself. *Got to keep my priorities straight.*

But that thought, like the potential waiting voice message, felt like a bomb tucked away in some long forgotten place, ticking down and waiting to explode.

Chapter Five

T he Hix residence was about eleven miles away from the
Hopkinses' address. Located just outside of the Frankfield city
limits, it was close enough to the town to offer Bannerman and his
crew authority over the case. Chicago loomed just twenty minutes
to the south, giving the section between something of a gray area
when it came to jurisdiction. The neighborhood was a little less
extravagant than the Hopkinses', though not by much. The yards
were smaller, most of them separated from the next by towering
elms and oaks. In the falling rain, the trees made the houses and
their yards look a little gothic as Kate and DeMarco pulled into the
Hixes' driveway.

DeMarco used they key Bannerman had given them to enter.
From what they had been told, the husband had moved just up the
road to Chicago, to stay with his brother directly after the funeral.
There was no indication as to when he might return.

However, not too long after Kate and DeMarco had allowed
themselves in, another car pulled into the driveway behind them.
The agents waited at the door to see who the visitor was. They
watched as a middle-aged blonde woman got out of a very nice
Mercedes. Kate noted that the car had Realtor plates.

"Hey there," the woman—presumably a Realtor—said as
she neared the stairs. She was clearly confused. "Can I ask who
you are?"

Kate flashed her badge, not being showy but also not wanting
to beat around the bush. "Agents Wise and DeMarco, FBI. You're a
Realtor, I take it?"

"That's right. Nadine Owen. I'm here to give the house a final walkthrough before we put it on the market."

"I wasn't aware it was going on the market," Kate said.

"We got the call yesterday morning. Mr. Hix won't be returning. He's got a moving crew coming in tomorrow to start packing everything up. I'm doing a checklist today to make sure the moving crew leaves it as is. Lord knows it'll be a hard enough sell as it is."

"Why is that?" DeMarco asked.

Kate knew the answer, having been involved in several cases in the past where a Realtor had come into play. "Realtors have to disclose when there has been a recent murder on a property," Kate said.

"That's right," Nadine said. "And in this case, Mr. Hix is donating just about everything he has. He was a mess when I spoke with him. He just doesn't want all of the reminders of his wife in whatever place he chooses as his next home. It's quite sad, actually."

That's pretty suspicious if you ask me, Kate thought.

"How long has Mr. Hix been in Chicago?" she asked.

"He left the day after the funeral...so I'd say three days, I believe."

"If you don't mind, we'd like to look the place over before you go about your checklist," Kate said.

"By all means."

The three women entered the house. Kate found it in immaculate shape. Again, it wasn't quite as nice as the Hopkins home, but it was still more than Kate would ever have been able to afford. It wasn't just the house, either; all of the furniture looked to be very expensive as well.

As they walked through, DeMarco trailed behind Kate, scrolling through the electronic police reports. She read aloud the important parts as they did a walkthrough of the house.

"Marjorie Hix was found dead in her bedroom, half in and half out of the master bathroom," she read. "She, too, was choked to death but there was no blood or cuts as there were with Karen Hopkins. There was bruising around her throat but no signs of hand imprints. It is believed she might have been strangled with a belt or some sort of smooth rope."

The downstairs was mostly an open floor plan, the living room and kitchen separated only by one large column. The other area appeared to serve as the living room, a small but expensive-looking television situated between two bookshelves. An elegant-looking piano also helped to separate the areas. Kate knew very little about pianos but was fairly certain this one was a baby grand Steinway ... and that it was likely valued at one year of her salary. It was hard to imagine the husband simply donating such an item rather than selling it. It sent a little red flag up in Kate's brain.

A reading area and mini-office space sat to the far left, tucked in a corner and looking out onto a spacious porch via a picture window. All in all, it looked rather plain and idyllic.

"Remind me again what the reports say about evidence taken by the police," Kate said.

"The husband willingly handed over his own laptop, which was given back pretty quickly," DeMarco said, still reading from the reports. "He also handed over Marjorie's laptop and cell phone. There was a belt in the upstairs closet that was taken in by forensics as a potential murder weapon, but it was conclusively determined *not* to have been used."

After a bit more looking downstairs, they walked up the stairs on the right side of the floor plan, the stairs running parallel to the little office space. The upstairs consisted of a wide hall and four rooms: a bathroom, two guest rooms, and a massive master suite. They went directly to the master suite and stopped just inside the doorway, taking the place in.

The bed was unmade, but other than that the room was spotless. Kate looked to the area in front of the bathroom and tried to picture a body there. She knew the crime scene photos were in the case files and she was sure she'd look at them later. For now, though, she was trying to picture the room like a killer might—a killer who had likely been invited in for some reason or another.

The room was situated in a way where someone coming out of the bathroom would not immediately see someone coming into the room. If the killer had managed to sneak into the room while Marjorie Hix had been in the bathroom, he would have gone completely unseen.

"No clues of any kind in the bedroom, huh?" Kate asked.

"None listed in the report. Not even a single drop of blood. Nothing."

Kate walked around the room and stopped at the window closest to the bed. She had to draw the curtains back, but she saw that it looked out onto a back yard with a wooded lot beyond. She then went into the bathroom. It, like most everything else in the house, was large and boastful. She hunkered down on her haunches and peered beneath the little thin spaces between the bottoms of the counters under the sinks and the floor. Other than a few stray dust bunnies, there was nothing.

"What's the security system like?" Kate asked.

"Um," DeMarco said as she scanned through the reports. "Apparently, there's no actual security system. But they do have one of those doorbell cameras."

"That's perfect. Did the PD get access to it?"

"Yes. It says here that the husband gave Bannerman the passcode. Apparently, it's all accessible through the camera's mobile app."

"Any idea what the app is?"

"It doesn't say. I'm sure Bannerman has it, though."

"Hold that thought," Kate said. She left the bedroom with DeMarco trailing behind her, still scrolling through the records.

They found Nadine Owen checking over the living room walls, apparently looking for preexisting scuff marks before the movers arrived. "Ms. Owen," Kate said. "Would you happen to know the name of the app the Hixes used for their doorbell camera?"

"I do, actually," she said. "When the husband called to list the house, he gave me their passcode so I could go in and kill the account before someone else moved in."

"Have you killed it yet?"

"No." Nadine seemed to understand where this was all headed. A look of brief excitement crossed her face as she pulled out her cell phone. "I can log in under his account if you need to check it."

"That would be great," Kate said.

Nadine sat down at one of the barstools along the kitchen counter and opened up the app. Kate and DeMarco watched as Nadine logged in under the Hix account. Within a few seconds, the address of the Hix home popped up. Nadine clicked on it and a page with a calendar appeared on the screen.

"The app allows us to go back sixty days. Anything more than that and it all gets stored on the cloud."

"Sixty days is more than enough. In fact, there are just two days I need you to check."

"I assume one would be from eight days ago, right? The day she was killed?"

"Yes, please."

"How exactly does this work?" DeMarco asked.

"There's a sensor on the doorbell," Nadine said. "When anyone comes up on the porch, it activates the camera. It then records until the person is either inside the house or has otherwise left the porch."

"So there will only be a video entry on the day of her murder if someone walked up on the porch, correct?" Kate asked.

"That's right. And … here we are. There are two videos from last Wednesday … the day she was killed."

The three women hunched around Nadine's phone, watching the somewhat grainy color playback from the app's video feed. The first video was easy to dismiss right away. It was a UPS driver, placing a box on the front porch and then quickly walking away and returning to his truck. The box was not very large and was adorned with the Amazon logo on the side. Three seconds after the driver was gone, the camera cut off.

Nadine then pulled up the second video and pressed Play. A woman came up onto the porch and rang the doorbell. It was answered several seconds later. There was no audio, but it was clear the woman on the porch was conversing with whoever had answered the door—presumably Marjorie. This was made clear a few moments later when Marjorie stepped out onto the porch, chatted with the woman for about a minute, and headed back inside. The woman called something out over her shoulder as she went down the stairs, and then the video was done.

"Any idea who that woman is?" DeMarco asked Nadine.

"No, sorry. Now, you said there was some other date you needed to check out?"

"Yes. Exactly two weeks ago. Are there any entries there?"

Nadine did some scrolling and then stopped when the calendar stopped fourteen days ago. There were two entries that day as well. Nadine played the first one right away, without being asked to do so.

Instantly, Kate recognized the man who came up onto the porch, ringing the doorbell: Mike Wallace. He was wearing the same Hexco uniform they had seen him in less than an hour ago. After several seconds, the door was answered, he spoke to someone for about ten seconds, and was then invited inside.

Nadine looked to them both, as if to see if there was any reaction. When she saw that there was none, she tapped at the next entry—particularly at the time stamp. "This next one is only fourteen minutes later."

She pressed play and they watched as the exact opposite of what they had just seen happened. Mike Wallace came out of the front door, back into the frame. He turned and spoke to someone at the door—again, presumably Marjorie Hix. The conversation lasted about twenty seconds and then Mike headed down the stairs. Before Mike's exit had a chance to kill the feed, the little sensor picked up more movement. Marjorie Hix stepped out onto the porch with a watering can and set to watering a pot of lilacs on the porch rail.

While it didn't prove much, the fact that there were no security videos of Mike Wallace on the day of her death was a pretty strong alibi.

"Anything else?" Nadine asked.

Kate and DeMarco shared a look and they both shook their heads simultaneously. Kate wasn't sure if DeMarco was thinking the same thing she was or not, but she knew there was a good chance.

The security footage had basically ruled out Mike Wallace. But the husband …

"There's a garage on the side of the property," Kate said. "Looks like it's on some sort of sublevel to the house, is that right?"

"It is. Would you like to see it?"

"No, that's not necessary. But would you happen to know if that's where Mr. Hix always parked?"

"I'm fairly certain, yes."

"And I assume there's a primary entrance into the house through that garage?"

"Of course." She pointed to a door at the very back of the house, just off of the kitchen and inside a mudroom area. "Right there."

So he would never even have to go past that doorbell sensor, Kate thought.

So while the videos had ruled out Mike Wallace, they had done nothing to help stave off her suspicions of the husband.

Kate looked back into the den—to the furniture, the knick-knacks, and other expensive items. She found it hard to think that someone would just abandon it all.

"Would you happen to know where Mr. Hix is staying?"

And in that, Nadine continued to be very helpful.

CHAPTER SIX

It appeared as though Marjorie Hix's husband—fifty-three-year-old Joseph Hix—had done much better for himself than his brother. Whereas Joseph Hix had managed a home in an affluent suburb and, according to the police reports, worked a job that had netted nearly four hundred thousand dollars the year before, his brother, Kyle, was living in a rather rundown apartment complex. It was located in an okay part of town, separate from a not-so-okay part of town by only a few blocks.

The apartment building had been constructed to look as if the open breezeways containing stairs separated little townhouses, but Kate had seen enough of these types of complexes to know that was not the case. The walked up two flights of the stairs and came to Kyle Hix's apartment. Kate knocked on the door, not expecting an answer.

So when it was answered almost right away, she was surprised. Not only that, but it was answered in such a loud and abrasive way that she jumped back a bit, nearly going for her gun.

The man who answered the door looked out of his mind—exhausted, angry to have been disturbed, and squinting from the sunlight.

"Who're you?" the man asked.

"Are you Joseph Hix?" Kate asked.

He grunted, as if he wasn't too sure of this himself. It was also clear that he had no intention of answering. As she waited, Kate caught a whiff of alcohol—something strong. Whiskey, she thought.

DeMarco took out her ID first, then Kate followed suit. Kate let DeMarco take the lead, always trying to remain aware that part of her special arrangement with Duran and the bureau could also be a great training opportunity for DeMarco.

"Agents DeMarco and Wise," DeMarco said. "We're on location in Frankfield, looking into the murder of your wife."

The man nodded and stepped away from the door. He swayed a bit when he did, making Kate wonder if that whiff of whiskey had been from a very recent drink—and here it was, not even two in the afternoon yet.

"Well, yeah…I'm Joseph. And I could have saved you the trip. I can tell you who killed her. Come on in…I'll help you out." He grinned, apparently amusing himself, and headed back inside.

"Whoa, hold on," DeMarco said. "You can't just make a statement like that. Do you for sure know who killed her?"

"I have no proof, but I have a damned good idea."

"Maybe you let us be the judges of that," Kate said. "What do you have?"

"I'll show you."

They followed him inside and Kate started to feel a bit uneasy. She wasn't sure if Hix was in a perpetual state of grief and drunkenness or if he was a little off the rails—or both. But what she did know was men handled grief very differently. And the tired, I-don't-give-a-shit look she had seen when he opened the door never led to anything good.

The apartment was modestly furnished but was limited in space. Hix led them directly to the kitchen, where he didn't even bother trying to seem like a well-adjusted guy. He grabbed a bottle of whiskey that had been sitting on the counter and poured himself a tumbler. He shrugged to the agents and downed it in one gulp.

"It doesn't bring her back," he said with a grimace, "but it makes it hurt a hell of a lot less."

"This is your brother's place, right?" Kate asked.

"Yeah. It's a shithole, but Kyle…he's all I got now."

"Mr. Hix, would you be willing to answer some questions for us?"

"Yeah. But like I said, I can tell you who killed her. I told the cops, too…but you see how far that got me."

Kate didn't want to take his bait, not wanting to let a grief-stricken and drunk man lead them down a rabbit hole that would likely go nowhere. Apparently, DeMarco felt the same because when she asked her next question, she did her best to veer the conversation elsewhere.

"You work as a proposal specialist, right?" DeMarco asked. "Something with telecom?"

"Yes. They've given me two months...like it's a favor. I work sixty hours almost every week and stay in France for them at least two months total out of every year."

"Did it strain your marriage?" Kate asked.

Hix nodded and pulled the bottle back to him. He looked at it longingly, desperate for another shot. She could see him considering it.

"Of course it did. She was unhappy most of the time, I guess. She acted like she was happy when I was actually around and never got too confrontational when I was away so much. At the risk of sounding like a bastard, she enjoyed the money. She always joked about it, but there was a whole lot of truth to it, you know? And there seemed to be a lot more joking after our son was gone."

"Gone?"

"Yeah...as soon as he left for college, things seemed to get a little more tense."

"How long ago was that?"

"Nine or ten years. Don't get me wrong...we loved each other very much. I don't know how that woman loved me as much as she did, but..."

He decided to go ahead and take that other shot. He did it as if he were set on a mechanical spring, going through the actions like someone with far too much practice.

"We always talked about taking trips after he was gone. Rome, Sydney, Madrid...those were the big ones. But I think she knew they'd never happen; it would take too much commitment on my part."

Listening to him talk, Kate was reminded of the call she had ignored from Melissa. It made her feel bad, as she wondered if the issues Melissa and Terry had been having were similar. Of course, neither of them made enough money to promise trips to one another, but an absentee spouse was an absentee spouse no matter how you cut it. Inexplicably, she felt the need to speak with Melissa quite badly in that moment.

But DeMarco, getting very adept at questioning potential suspects, kept the ball rolling quickly and efficiently.

"Were you at work when Marjorie was murdered?"

"I was. I was actually on a flight back from Seattle. I'd been there on business for three days. I landed at O'Hare and got a barrage of missed calls and texts from the police before I even got off of the plane."

"You claim to know who did it," DeMarco went on. "Did you think you knew even then?"

"More or less, yes. But now, almost a week afterwards without a single suspect, I become more and more certain."

"And who might you have in mind as the suspect?"

"A guy named Andrew Bauer."

"And why do you think he did it?"

"Because he's always had a thing for Marjorie ... ever since they graduated college and found out they were living less than ten minutes away from one another. The guy is a sleazebag. I know it might sound pretentious and judgmental, but I don't care—the guy is single and living in a neighborhood that is predominantly married couples with children. And he's at home for days on end, sort of just stalking around the neighborhood and befriending all of the lonely women who have men that work long hours."

"And how do you know this?"

"It's pretty common knowledge. Andrew is a pilot. He works a few days, he's home a few days. I'm not the only man in the neighborhood that had to have a word with him."

"What sort of word?" Kate asked.

"About a year ago, I came home and found him standing in my yard while Marjorie was pulling weeds in her flowerbed. He had this evil grin on his face. I don't know how to explain it. He's just slimy."

"How does that equate to him potentially killing your wife?" DeMarco asked.

"I suspected an affair. I had ever since that day. Marjorie denied it, of course, but there were small signs. She'd wash the sheets a lot more than usual. She'd start sort of trash talking Andrew a little too much—and it came out of nowhere, like she was trying to cover something up."

"Did you ever confront her on it?"

"Almost. We had an argument about four months ago when she wasn't…well, when she wasn't active in the bedroom. We'd never had that problem but whenever I would try to start something spontaneous, she'd shoot me down. And that had *never* been like her."

"Did you ever confront him about it?"

"No. But damn, I wish I had."

"So you think…what?" Kate asked.

"I think he got pissed at her because she wouldn't leave me for him."

"With all due respect," DeMarco said, "that's a very large stretch."

"I'm well aware of that. But at the same time, there *is* such a thing as a husband's intuition—though women don't like to hear it, no offense. I just had a feeling about him. And it's stronger now."

DeMarco nodded and Kate watched as Hix took yet another shot of whiskey. "Well, Mr. Hix, we'll look into him. We can't accuse him of something like you are suggesting. But we can question him because, based on this moment you saw him in your yard, he seemed to have been at least friendly with your wife."

"That's one way of putting it," Hix said, and then took the shot. He came around the counter of the little kitchen counter, having to hold on to it to keep from wobbling. "And by the way, it wasn't just Marjorie. He moved to our neighborhood several years ago because he had been caught having an affair with another man's wife, somewhere here in town, in Chicago."

Kate and DeMarco started back for the front door. Hix stumbled slowly after them, doing his best to seem hospitable in an apartment that was not his own. Kate paused at the door as DeMarco opened it. She turned back to Hix, who was visibly swaying on his feet.

"Mr. Hix…is there someone we can call for you?" she asked. "I'm sure you know there are all sorts of support groups to help you with this."

"And I intend to go to one, eventually," he said. "But I have to have closure first. Until that bastard is brought down, I can't…it'll just be me, my brother, and bottle after bottle."

"We'll try to wrap this up as quickly as possible, then."

She tore her eyes away from him, the sight of his blurred eyes and hopeless expression far beyond haunting. She'd seen many men grieving before but she had always personally mourned for those who turned to substance abuse as a way to cope.

He waved them away half-heartedly as they walked out onto the porch. Kate turned to get one more look at him, hoping maybe there might be some sense of hope on his face before they left, but Hix had already shut the door behind them.

CHAPTER SEVEN

"I just want to make sure we're on the same page before we go speak to this Andrew Bauer guy," DeMarco said.

"Okay," Kate said. "What are your thoughts?"

"I think Hix was just trying to pin the murder on someone so he'd have some hope of closure."

"We think the same thing, then. Although I won't completely discount the speculation about the affair. And that's really the only reason I think we need to speak with him."

They'd placed a call to Bannerman upon leaving Chicago on their way back to Frankfield. After he gave them the address for Andrew Bauer, DeMarco had called the airport, found out which airline Bauer flew for, then requested his schedule. It had all taken less than fifteen minutes; by the time they were entering Frankfield, they had confirmation that Bauer was not on duty for another two days.

They found themselves heading back into the neighborhood where Marjorie Hix had been murdered. It almost felt like coming full circle as they passed the Hix home—the very same home they'd been in less than two hours ago.

Andrew Bauer's home was three blocks farther down and to the right. It was one of the smaller homes in the neighborhood but the yard looked immaculately cared for. In fact, as Kate pulled their car to the curb in front of the home, they saw a man standing in front of the house, hard at work. From what Kate could tell, he was laying down paver stones to separate the yard from the flowerbeds and other landscaping. He was tearing up what looked like old wooden planks and replacing them with the stones. The man was dressed in gym shorts and a tank top. He was perhaps fifty years old but had a toned body the tank top did little to hide. His shoulders were massive and the sweat from the tank top clung to his well-defined torso.

"See?" DeMarco said. "Moments like this, I'm very glad I like women. Men like that… they can't be anything but trouble, right?"

Kate smirked as she opened the car door. Yes, this man—presumably Andrew Bauer—was incredibly good-looking. But such a facade had stopped having any effect on her years ago.

They approached Bauer, striding up the sidewalk. Bauer was in the middle of laying down a paver stone, looking up at them as he set it in place.

"Mr. Andrew Bauer?" Kate said.

"Yeah," he said with a grunt. "That's me. Can I help you?"

Kate showed her badge and ran through introductions. She noted that when she said *"FBI,"* he looked slightly alarmed.

"Oh yeah?" he said. "Am I…in trouble or something? What's up?"

"We wanted to ask you a few questions about Marjorie Hix."

Bauer finished with the stone, wiped his hands on his shorts, and stood up. He looked relieved now, albeit a bit confused. "Marjorie?"

"Yes. We're told you knew her."

"Sure I did. She lives a few blocks that way," he said, pointing behind them. "Or *lived*, I guess. Pretty terrible about what happened to her."

"You know anything about *what* happened to her?" DeMarco asked.

"No. And I'll tell you the same thing I told the police when they came by asking. It's terrible that someone killed Marjorie but I don't like the fact that the delusional husband assumed it was me."

"Did you have a friendship with Joseph Hix?" Kate asked.

"No. He's basically hated me ever since I moved into town. And he's not the only one, really. But Joseph's thing against me was more of a jealousy thing. I knew her back in college, you see. And we sort of had this unofficial thing."

"These other men not liking you," Kate said. "Does that have anything to do with the affair you left behind when you left Chicago?"

"It might. I don't really know—don't really care. But someone in the neighborhood heard about it and just because I'm single, it makes me a threat. It's a little pathetic. If these men wouldn't spend half their lives in an office, maybe they wouldn't worry about their wives straying."

"Did you have an affair with Marjorie Hix after college?" Kate asked bluntly.

"No. And I'd hardly call it an affair in college. We never slept together. Just some flirting and a few nights where things almost happened."

"So would you explain the day Joseph Hix came home and found you standing in his yard, talking to his wife?"

"Yeah. Again, like I told the cops, I was out for a run. I was passing by their house and Marjorie was out in the yard, doing something with the flowerbeds—weeding, I guess, because she was struggling to get this jug of weed killer open. I asked if she needed some help and she gratefully accepted. I opened it for her and we talked about the best way to weed flowerbeds. We did some reminiscing about college, too. That led to her asking why I had moved to town, and me telling her about this job I had landed in Chicago. It was friendly conversation and nothing more. I just happened to be there, in the yard, when her husband pulled up. And ever since that evening, he's made a hobby out of dragging my name through the mud."

"And did you have any conversations with her after that?" DeMarco asked.

"Yeah. And some of them made me uncomfortable. It got to the point where I felt like she had learned my schedule. She knew when I wasn't working and figured out when I went on my runs—right around four in the afternoon."

"What made you uncomfortable about the conversations?"

"She'd start griping about how her husband was a workaholic. It was weird, the way she just sort of opened up to me. She didn't even get that deep when we were back in college. She seemed desperate to talk to someone. I don't know. If I'm being honest…yeah, I liked the attention. There was no real flirting but…you know…just conversations a married woman should not be having with a single man."

"And it never got physical?"

"No."

"Did it get intimate in any way at all?" DeMarco asked.

"No. In fact, there was one day where she asked if I could take down her number, to maybe call when I had a free afternoon. I didn't do it, though. By then, I knew people had started suspecting me of being this home-wrecking asshole—from what I did in Chicago and from Joseph Bauer making things up."

"And how did you hear about her murder?" Kate asked.

"We have a neighborhood Facebook page. One of their neighbors posted it, warning everyone to keep their doors locked."

"Did you reach out to Joseph?"

"Honestly, I thought about it. But I decided in the end that it would probably be a very bad idea."

"Do you have an alibi for the day she was murdered?"

"I do. I was piloting a flight between Dallas and Seattle. You're fully welcome to check my flight schedule."

Kate nodded, this last bit making her feel as if they had wasted their time even coming out here. "By any chance, do you know a woman by the name of Karen Hopkins?"

He thought for a moment and then shook his head. "No, I don't think so. Does she live around here, in the neighborhood?"

"No," DeMarco said. "Mr. Bauer, if necessary, would you willingly allow us to pull up your phone records over the past year or so?"

"Why? To prove I wasn't sleeping with Marjorie Hix? It would be a pain in my ass, but yes, I'd gladly do it if it would prove that I had nothing to do with her—much less her murder."

"We may reach out to you for that," Kate said, though she was fairly certain it would not come to that. If Andrew Bauer had something as solid as a flight itinerary to prove his whereabouts on the day Marjorie Hix was killed, she was quite sure he had nothing to do with it.

They thanked him for his time and headed back for the car. She noted that Bauer had not returned to his work, but instead, had sat down on the front porch steps to rest. He watched them go and gave a small perfunctory wave before looking back to his handiwork.

It was nearing four o'clock, when Kate and DeMarco returned to the Frankfield PD. With no suspects or leads, Kate could not help but feel discouraged and maybe even a little defeated as they made their way back to Bannerman's office. They had not been assigned any certain room yet so Kate assumed Bannerman's office would serve as their base of operations.

Bannerman was not in his office, but the door was open. A bit awkwardly, they made their way inside and sat in the two chairs on the opposite side of Bannerman's seat. Kate simply relaxed a bit into the chair while DeMarco started tapping notes into her Notes app on her phone.

"At least we're starting to see some similarities in the victims," Kate said.

"Yeah," DeMarco agreed. "At first, I thought it was that they were in rocky marriages. But I think now, in both cases, it's safe to say they simply had disinterested husbands. Husbands that put them second below work."

"Seems like a pretty defined trait for a killer to pinpoint. But I'd take it one step further. Yes, they were both essentially afterthoughts to their husbands, and I think that could be boiled down to one single, more relatable trait."

"Which is?"

"They were lonely."

DeMarco considered this for a moment, nodding. "And a lonely middle-aged wife might be a little more prone to having a visitor ... someone they might invite inside."

"But it still gets tripped up when we consider the Hixes' little doorbell monitor."

"Yes, and I'm sure there are ways around that monitor."

"But *why* would you need a way around it if you weren't hiding something?"

"You think Marjorie Hix *was* having an affair?" Kate asked.

"I don't know. But ... at the risk of sounding stereotypical, aren't affairs a dime a dozen in neighborhoods like these?"

Kate shrugged. It *was* stereotypical but only because, as far as she had seen in the course of her career, it was backed by some pretty jarring facts and statistics.

In the middle of their brainstorming, Bannerman came walking into the room. DeMarco got up quickly, but Kate remained in her seat—not out of being impolite but because she thought she had Bannerman pegged pretty well. He'd appreciate that they were kicked back so comfortably in his office. It built camaraderie; it let him know that Kate was at ease in his presence. It tended to mean quite a lot to men of the law in their later years.

"Did I break up a meeting?" he asked with a smile. He sat down behind his desk as if he were programmed to do so. There were many years of experience in just that motion alone.

"Not a very productive one," Kate said.

"No luck today, I take it?"

"Not really. Hey ... did you speak to a guy named Andrew Bauer, at the strong suggestion of Joseph Hix?"

"I did," he said, frowning. "Shit. I didn't even bother putting it into the reports. I didn't think there was anything to it."

"I don't think there is," Kate said. "I think Hix was just looking for something easy to pin the murder on. He needs closure to move in from this."

"And from more than a bottle of whiskey," DeMarco added.

"Sheriff, maybe you can help us ... three heads are often better than two. The only real trait we have from the two victims that match up is the fact that they had marriages that left them feeling lonely. But there is no strong evidence of an affair. Who would these women so willingly allow into their homes? In the case of the Hix residence, someone who would be allowed in *and* bypassing their security measures at the front door?"

"That's where I got hung up," he admitted. "And I'll admit… I've got a police force that's about ninety percent male. So assuming there was adultery involved could have made us look…"

"Like jerks?" DeMarco said, though with a bit of a smile.

"Pretty much."

"But if there was some sort of fooling around or even just hiding a man for the pure conversation and proximity," Kate said, "it was not Andrew Bauer. I'm pretty sure of that."

Bannerman nodded his agreement. "Yeah, when we talked to Gerald Hopkins, he was not at all familiar with the name Andrew Bauer. That's why I dismissed him so easily."

"When we spoke with Bauer, he indicated that he felt that Marjorie Hix might have had a crush or something similar," Kate said. "He said he felt she just wanted someone to talk to at first and it was like she was purposefully waiting for him some days. It makes me wonder, if it's true, if there were more men in her life like that."

"Like what?" Bannerman asked.

"Men she used simply for the conversation. For a man that would speak to her and maybe look at her in the way her husband wasn't any longer. Like an emotional affair rather than a physical one."

"It's a big neighborhood," Bannerman said. "I'm sure there could be numerous men that would fit that description."

"We only singled out Bauer because of Hix's anger and the fact that he was single," DeMarco said. "And let's face it… being married doesn't always stop people from getting involved with other people that aren't their spouses."

It was an interesting thought—one that Kate focused on and tried to pick apart as she sat in Bannerman's chair. But try as she might, there was one other thing that kept creeping back to the center of her mind.

The missed call from Melissa.

The voicemail that was surely waiting.

Until she checked it, she would not be able to give this case her full attention.

She got to her feet and excused herself for the restroom. Even before she was completely out of Bannerman's office, she was reaching for her phone.

The message from Melissa had not been nearly as bad as Kate had been expecting. It had stung a bit, sure. It had made her feel about three inches tall, yes. But at the end of the day, Kate was glad that she'd checked the message and saw—for the first time in a long time—that her daughter still had some grit to her.

Kate could still hear fragments of it in her head as she sat at the Frankfield Inn's little bar area. DeMarco was beside her, chatting up the bartender, while Kate sipped on a beer and thought about Melissa and Michelle. Kate tried to distract herself with trying to determine if DeMarco and the rather pretty short-haired female bartender were flirting, but it wasn't working. There was just too much going on in her head.

"I don't know how you could be so irresponsible, Mom. Yes, Alan is a great guy and Michelle loves him. But I asked you to do this one thing for me... this one fucking thing... and you dropped it the moment a call came from DC. I don't know why I'm so surprised... not really. It's always been this way. Work before me. Work before Dad. So why the hell should I expect any different when it comes to your granddaughter?"

She was torn about how to feel because the truth of the matter was that in one sense, Melissa was right: she *had* always put career first. But to say that Melissa had never asked much of her was a little out of line. Of course, life had dealt her a shitty hand when her father had died and Kate had caught a lot of the burden of a grieving college student, already pissed at the world and scared about her future. But still... it was unfair for Melissa to claim she'd never done anything for her...

... I asked you to do this one thing for me ... this one fucking thing ...

It was amazing to find that her daughter could both enrage and sadden her at the same time. It was almost like she was reliving the teenage years all over again.

It also made her think of the two dead women, Karen Hopkins and Marjorie Hix. Women who had been overlooked and underappreciated by those who loved them. While on the surface it might make her appear to be spoiled, Kate could identify. In many ways, Melissa underappreciated her. She took her for granted and only came around or called when she needed something.

"Spill it, Wise."

Kate snapped out of her thoughts and looked over at DeMarco. She was no longer speaking with the bartender, though the bartender seemed to be keeping an eye on DeMarco. She was quite pretty, in a plain sort of way, with a thin tattoo of some sort of vine trailing down her arm.

"Spill what?"

"I'd hoped you would have realized by now that I'm pretty good at my job. And sometimes I notice a thing or two. You got a call this morning that you ignored right away. You've been somewhat distracted today. In Bannerman's office, you left very quickly and were grabbing for your phone right away. Everything okay at home? With Melissa? With Alan?"

"You *are* good. And I'm mostly fine. Just realizing that this case is sort of paralleling some of my personal life. Not in the murders, of course, but ... I don't know. These women weren't appreciated."

"And you don't feel like you are either?"

"Only when it comes to Melissa. Which sounds stupid, because really, why would I expect her to show her appreciation *all* the time?"

"Um, because you're her mother."

Kate shrugged and sipped from her beer. "It's just another one of those things that makes me think this was a mistake—that I should have just stayed retired."

"Kate ... I think a great deal of you. If we were just a little bit closer, I'd go so far as to say I love you. But do you realize that this is a complaint that you've had on the last few cases we've worked together?"

"Yeah, I know…"

"My own mother was okay and I'm mostly fine speaking to her these days," DeMarco said. "Moms and daughters don't always jive, you know? So I say you either just face the shit head on or make the decision that you're still your own woman—a bad-ass one, I might add—and you want to give your all to this job for the next few years. *Then* you can finally actually retire and be a grandmother." She chuckled here and added: "But damn, I hate to even think of you as being a *grandma*."

"Yeah…but age gets us all in the end."

When DeMarco gave her a sympathetic little frown and then turned away, Kate appreciated it. As a good partner, she could tell when Kate did not want to talk about something. And feeling that level of appreciation made Kate then think about Alan and the subtle little ultimatum he had given her. Kate had never been the type of woman to take ultimatums from anyone. So why had she so willingly listened to and accepted Alan's?

I'm just going to have to start setting better boundaries, she thought. *Not just for me and the job, but for my loved ones and my job, too.*

Chapter Eight

M eredith's husband had left for work an hour and a half ago, and she knew she had a long day of doing nothing but waiting for him to come back home. She was also excited that he'd be coming home early. Every now and then he'd get a day where there was nothing to do around his office. On those days, David would leave for work late and come home early, just heading in to make sure there were no immediate fires he had to put out. He usually left for work around 6:30 in the morning, but he'd stayed until 7:45 this morning. It had given them time for a quick morning-time romp in the bedroom and then a shower for him while she brewed coffee.

She was enjoying her second cup of coffee when she started to think about the day ahead. She and David were going to her favorite Italian restaurant and then they would go into the city for an art exhibit David was excited about. She sometimes joked with him about how he preferred to live just outside of Chicago rather than in the city, as most of the things he was interested in were there and not in their tired little home of Frankfield. David's plan was to start their life here, quietly, and have a few kids before moving into the city. They were both aware that most couples did it the other way—starting off a marriage in the city and the moving to the outskirts to raise their kids. But David had never been one for convention, and it was one of the many reasons she loved him.

They'd been married for just a little over a year, managing to land the respectable little home thanks to David finally landing his dream job as a copy editor with a growing publishing house. She was well aware that most twenty-four-year-old women with only a community college associate's degree were not as lucky to have the life she had, and she cherished it.

She also knew that David, nearly twenty years her senior, got a lot of grief about having robbed the cradle. But they were both fine with it; they had nestled out a pleasant little life for themselves. Yes, Meredith had her secrets that she kept from him, but she was pretty sure he had a few of his own as well.

She finished up her coffee and had started tidying up the kitchen when the doorbell rang. She was expecting company, so it did not take her by surprise. She went to the door and answered it, smiling politely at the man on the other side.

"Hey there," she said. "Come on in."

He was dressed in a basic black T-shirt and a pair of jeans. He had a small backpack slung over his right shoulder presumably to hold his tools and gadgets. "Sorry I'm late," he said.

"Oh, no worries at all."

"Based on the conversation we had, I don't see it taking too long."

"Great."

She led him down the main hallway, toward the den. As they walked, she spoke up—mainly because she had never been one to tolerate awkward silences.

"You know, I found it odd that you weren't listed online anywhere. I only knew about you because of the business card I saw on one of those business bulletin boards at the gym."

"I just prefer it this way," he said. "I don't trust much of anything online. And I hate answering emails. It's just easier this way."

"Yeah? You stay pretty busy?"

"As busy as I need."

"Good," she said, starting to wonder if maybe she should have done some more research before hiring him. He wasn't creeping her out by any means, but he was a little off-putting. She wasn't sure why; it was no specific thing she could put her finger on.

They came to the den, where she stood to the side and gestured inside. "Well, there you go. If you need anything, let me know."

"Will do. Thanks again."

"Thank *you!*"

She walked back into the kitchen, opening up the fridge and compiling a grocery list in her head. She worked from home as a freelance virtual assistant, but she was between clients right now and was having a hard time finding more work. Until she found more clients, she figured she'd do her best to assume the role of stay-at-home wife—something she never thought she would be but, in all reality, was sort of starting to enjoy.

She typed her grocery list down into the cute little app she used for daily tasks. Done with that, she set it down on the counter and started digging through the small recipe box she kept by the stove, planning to come up with a menu for the remainder of the week after tonight's date. As she was nearing the end of it, she heard something behind her. She turned and was startled to see the man she had let inside five minutes ago standing there.

"Did you need something else?" she asked.

"No. I was just wondering . . . where does your husband work?"

"Um . . . no offense, but I don't think that's your concern."

"Oh, no . . . nothing like that. I guess that *did* sound creepy. No, I saw a picture of him on the mantel in the den. He's standing by someone that looked very familiar in an office setting and I couldn't figure out who it is. It's driving me crazy."

"Oh!" Relief flooded through her; for a moment there, she had started to get freaked out. "He's a copy editor with Ember and Hudson Books. The other guy in that picture you're talking about is James Franco. They ran into one another a few months back at some meeting."

"Oh, that's so cool. Sorry . . . didn't meant to startle you."

"Oh, it's okay."

She turned her attention back to the grocery list, but apparently her guest was not done.

"Any kids?"

"No. Not yet."

"Yeah, I thought you looked rather young. Early twenties?"

The relief she'd felt moments ago disappeared completely and was replaced with something very much like dread.

"Yeah," she said. She glanced over to the phone on the counter. It was about ten feet away from her.

"This is a nice house," he said. "A lovely den, too. How long have you lived here?"

She reached out for the phone, not really caring if it seemed rude. She noted that his eyes followed her closely as she picked it up.

"Sorry," he said. "I do tend to get a little talkative. I'll get back to work."

She nodded and watched him go. When he was out of sight, she unlocked her phone and pulled up her recent texts. She pulled up the latest to David and started to type a new message. She started to pace, as she usually did when she got nervous about something. She tried to think of what to say, but never even got the chance to start properly. All she got out was: *The guy…*

But she got no further.

She felt something slip around her neck and then a very hard pressure against her spine. She didn't even have time to cry out. Whatever was around her neck pulled tight and she could not breathe. Her neck felt as if it were being pinched by a giant and at once, she started to struggle.

It did not last long, though.

Meredith fought for less than thirty seconds before darkness started to envelop everything she saw. Her phone slipped from her hands, clattering on the floor, her text to her husband incomplete and undelivered.

CHAPTER NINE

The Frankfield Inn's bar had been surprisingly good the night before, not just for drinks but for the food. It was not, however, open for breakfast or lunch. That's how Kate and DeMarco ended up at an IHOP the following morning, having an early breakfast after checking in to no results at the Frankfield PD. They pored over the case files as they sipped coffee and nibbled from massive breakfast plates that Kate knew would go mostly uneaten.

"No way you look at this do Karen Hopkins and Marjorie Hix seem alike in any way other than their age," DeMarco said. "Not in their professions, not their interests, not their contacts, nothing."

"Well, nothing except husbands that didn't value them," Kate pointed out.

"And if there were no affairs that we know of, what does that leave?"

"I think we may need to start looking into friends ... even passing acquaintances. Someone has to know a link. Someone would have to know what sort of friends Hopkins and Hix had coming in and out of their homes."

"It's that damned doorbell security system that's tripping me up," DeMarco said. "Whoever killed Marjorie Hix likely came in through the garage. The answer would be why."

"It could have been any number of reasons. Maybe it was someone who was actually in a car with Marjorie. They could have come back to her house together, Marjorie parked in the garage, and then they went into the house."

"You know, this would be much easier if these husbands took an interest in their wives," DeMarco joked.

Kate clung to the comment. She felt like, though it had been said in jest, there was something to it. Was there something there they were potentially missing? If the husbands did not keep up with their wives, what might those husbands be missing out on? Maybe it was more than just intimacy and attention. Maybe it was smaller things?

"I wonder," Kate said, "if there were smaller things in these women's lives that the husbands didn't even know about. If we dig *very* deep, could there be some small and seemingly inconsequential thing they shared in common? Something maybe linking them to the killer?"

"It's a great thought, but that takes us right back to finding someone who actually knew these women better than their husbands."

Kate realized that it did sort of create a very ragged circle with no end in sight. Still, she focused on that last comment, wondering if they had missed something smaller and almost invisible among the crime scenes. Something in the background that seemed of no consequence at first or even second glance.

She was about to say this out loud when her phone rang. She dug it out of her pocket and saw that it was Melissa. She was flooded with that mix of anger, resentment, and sorrow. She nearly ignored it right away but then remembered how distracted she had been yesterday. If she did not take this call, she'd wonder about it all day.

"I'm so sorry," she said, getting up from the table. "I have to take this."

DeMarco waved her away casually as she continued to read over the case notes. Kate made her way to the front doors, stepping outside onto the sidewalk in front of the restaurant as she answered the call.

"Hey, Lissa."

"Mom...I don't know what to do. I'm sorry to call, I really am, and I know I said some messed up things in that message yesterday but..."

"Calm down," Kate said. She worried that something else had happened between her and Terry. The protective mother in her wondered if Terry had left them or, even worse and more unimaginable, struck Melissa or Michelle. "Slow down and star over."

"Michelle is showing her symptoms again...when we had that cancer scare. Mom...what the hell do I do?"

"What's she doing?" Kate asked, trying to stay as calm as possible.

"When she cries, she screams. And it's exactly the same kind of screams as before, when I took her to the doctor and they saw those abnormalities."

"How long has she been doing it?"

"Since yesterday afternoon. And Mom...God, I'm so sorry. I blamed you. I blamed you and Alan, thinking he had fed her something he shouldn't and..."

"Melissa, it's okay. Look...that screaming was just one symptom, remember? What were some others?"

"There was a fever, but the doctors weren't even sure it was related."

"Melissa...when you picked her up from my house, was she fine?"

"Yes. She got a little upset when I started yelling at Alan, though."

"You yelled at Alan?"

"Mom, I was so pissed off. At you, at him, at myself..."

"Okay, fine. Look...if it's just screaming, treat it as if it were gas or colic. Honey, you can't assume every little thing that goes wrong is going back to where we were a few months ago. The doctors cleared her. You know that."

"I know, but..."

"Hasn't she always been a little fussy after she stays with me for a long period of time? Remember...we talked about this? Your little one does not like change. It throws her off. This sounds to me like nothing more than colic."

"Are you sure?"

Kate had no idea why, but this question angered her. Melissa sounded almost hysterical, paranoid, and nervous—wanting to ensure that her baby was fine. But at the same time, she also sounded hopeless and totally inept.

"Swaddle her in a blanket and then lay her flat on her belly. But just for a while and do *not* leave her. Make sure her face is turned to the side and rub her on the back. Do that for a while and then roll her over. Do it a few times. If she's still screaming after all of that and you need to just be sure, call the pediatrician."

"Mom, I don't know. I think it's more than gas and..."

"You've thought this twice since the scare, Melissa. And what did it turn out being both times?"

There was silence on the other end. Kate assumed the silence was the result of Melissa sneering on the other end. "The first time it was gas and the second time was mild reflux when we tried her on that new formula."

"Exactly."

"Mom, what if..."

"Melissa, I love you. And I will always love you. But you are a mother now. You can't come running to me with every problem. Especially when..."

She'd nearly ended that statement with *"especially when I'm working,"* but managed to stop herself.

But Melissa apparently knew how the statement was going to end. "Yeah, got it, Mom. Especially when..."

"Melissa, I—"

Her phone beeped at her as another call came in. She checked it and while she did not recognize the number, she did recognize the local area code.

"Melissa, I have another call I have to take."

"Of course you do."

Melissa ended the call, the slight click sending a shiver through Kate. She inhaled deeply, let it out, and then answered the other call. "This is Agent Wise."

"Agent Wise, it's Sheriff Bannerman. I need you and your partner to meet up with me as soon as possible."

Even before she asked the question that came out of her mouth, she knew what he would say. It was just a gut feeling she had, one that she had learned to trust early on in her career.

"We've got another body...a third victim."

CHAPTER TEN

Victim number three, a twenty-four-year-old named Meredith Lowell, lived in a cute little two-story home about three miles outside of Frankfield. When Kate and DeMarco pulled into the U-shaped driveway, an ambulance was pulling out the other end. There was a single cop car in the driveway, unoccupied. Bannerman stood on the porch at the front door, watching as the agents parked and got out of the car.

"What's with the ambulance?" Kate asked.

"The husband found the body. Came home from work early to surprise her and had a minor cardiac episode. He was in the back of the ambulance. He was wailing and crying as they put him in, poor guy."

"You the only officer on the scene?"

"I've got more on the way. I wanted you two to have access to the scene before anyone else."

"Thanks for that," Kate said as she and DeMarco joined him on the porch. Bannerman opened the door for them and they stepped inside.

It was the smallest home they had been in but it was still quite nice. The living room sat off of a small hallway on one side of the house and everything else sat on the opposite side. About halfway down the hall, a den sat off to the right. In front of them at the exact center of the home was a large kitchen.

The body of Meredith Lowell say on the floor, her head resting directly beside the dishwasher. Her eyes were wide open, staring up at the ceiling. Her blonde hair was tufted out around her head like a little halo. Right away, Kate could see the mark on her neck and knew this was not just a random murder. This was a third victim of the killer they were after.

Kate knelt down by the body on one side while DeMarco dropped to the other side. She studied the marks on Meredith's neck and saw right away that they were similar to the other victims. The marks on Meredith's neck were essentially just one mark, with a few areas where the strangulation weapon had drifted a bit. The indentation from the weapon was the same width as the others and although the area was red and swollen, there were no areas that were cut into as there had been with Karen Hopkins. There appeared to be no other signs of attack; the killer had clearly come in with the intention of strangling her.

"Did you manage to get anything out of the husband before he left?"

"Very little. He wanted to help, but the medics were too concerned about his health. They're going to let us know the moment he's okay for visitors. What I did get out of him, though, was sort of telling. He left for work later than usual, with plans to get home early. But he actually managed to leave work much earlier than he expected. He had intended to come home and surprise his wife, planning to take her to lunch, a movie, and then dinner. A nice little day date."

"So he wasn't gone long at all, right?"

"He said he was gone perhaps three hours and fifteen minutes."

"I think that gives us definitive proof that the killer is being invited in," Kate said. "Even if it was just someone who knew the family's schedule well, there's no way they could have known the husband was going to come back early."

"Could have just been luck," Bannerman suggested.

"This also breaks the connection we thought we had with the other victims," DeMarco said. "This woman is young."

"Twenty-four, by the husband's words," Bannerman said. "The husband was older, though. Maybe forty, if I had to guess."

"Any kids?" Kate asked.

"I don't think so," Bannerman said. "Not between the two of them, though this seems to be the husband's second marriage. But if she's this young and there are no kids here in the house right now, my guess would be no."

"You said you have units on the way?"

"About five minutes away by now, I'd think."

"Coroner?"

"Right behind my guys."

"Good. With this body so fresh, it should be easy for them to find out what was used to strangle her. And if we can figure that out and make sure it could be applicable to the other murders, that could be a huge help."

Kate got to her feet and started to slowly pace around the kitchen. She went to the back door, which led out to a cute little patio. No signs of a break-in, no signs of a struggle. Nothing. She then walked through the hallway and did a lap around the living room. From a quick first glance, nothing appeared to be missing or disturbed. She checked the front door and found it just as untouched as the back.

She walked through the den, taking the same approach. She looked over the furniture, the family-related items. There was a piano in the center of the room, a small writing desk tucked away in the corner, a beautiful acoustic Gibson guitar on a stand in another corner. Nothing disturbed, nothing removed.

Wait ... but there's something here. Some link ... what am I missing?

She could feel her intuition trying to bring something to the surface. She wanted to force it, but knew better. It would come soon enough. Still, she looked around the room one more time, trying to figure out what exactly was gnawing at her.

By the time she returned to the kitchen, the first of Bannerman's units showed up. And, as he had said, the coroner arrived directly behind them.

There were three other officers in all, looking the place over and running through routine procedure—checking for prints and essentially running through the same checklists Kate had just run through. But really, with the husband on the way to the hospital and no one to question, their jobs were over within a few minutes.

Kate and DeMarco stood by in the kitchen while the coroner snapped a few photos and examined the body. "Any idea what the killer used to strangle her?" DeMarco asked the coroner.

The coroner, a hardened woman who looked to be in her forties, gave a lazy shrug. "Hard to tell. I don't see any fibers or evidence of rope burn, so I'm going to rule out rope or twine right away. If I had to make a quick non-educated guess, I'd think it was some sort of craft string—maybe something plastic or made with a pliable sort of weak metal."

"Once you get her in, how long till you think you'd be able to give us a more accurate guess?"

"I can make it the priority of the case and maybe have something in a few hours."

The coroner looked to the string-like indentation and shook her head. She snapped a few more pictures as Kate and DeMarco stepped backward, giving her room.

"There were cuts on Karen Hopkins's neck," DeMarco said. "No cuts on Marjorie Hix, but a few abrasions. Maybe it's a different material each time?"

"That, or the killer is getting better at it and getting a better feel for how to do it."

"So he's coming in, knowing exactly what he's going to do and how he's going to get it done," DeMarco said. "And if he's also being invited in, he has the convenience of taking his time, waiting for his moment."

"What the hell are we missing?" Kate asked. She was starting to feel frustrated, looking back toward the den and wondering what had nibbled at her there.

"You know...so what if she's younger?" DeMarco said. "She's still a woman who was alone in a suburban house."

"Yes, but given the little we know about the husband, she wasn't a neglected and lonely wife. He was coming home early from work to take her on a day date. I'd say that's the exact opposite of the other two victims."

DeMarco nodded her understanding, looking back toward the kitchen where the coroner was wrapping up. As she was about to step back into the kitchen, her phone rang. She pulled her phone out, checked the display, and then looked oddly at Kate.

"What?" Kate asked.

"It's Duran." She waited a moment before answering and although it did seem like a very minor event, the weight of it was not missed by Kate. In the past, Duran had always called her to check up on a case or ask questions. She assumed it was because he had always viewed her as the lead, mentoring and bringing up DeMarco along the way.

Now, apparently, he was starting to see things differently, and Kate wasn't sure why. She stood silently and listened to DeMarco's end of the conversation, trying not to feel too jilted by it.

"This is DeMarco…yes, sir. Just now…about ten minutes. Sheriff Bannerman, yes sir." There was a lengthy pause here, where Kate could hear Duran's muffled voice through the phone but could make nothing out. When he was done, DeMarco responded with: "Understood."

DeMarco ended the call, a slight look of disappointment on her face.

"Everything okay?" Kate asked.

"Yes. He just found out about the victim. He said he'd called the coroner a few days ago and asked to be notified of any bodies related to our case."

"So he was checking up on us?"

DeMarco nodded, but found it hard to look at Kate.

"Correction," Kate said. "He was checking up on *me*, wasn't he?"

DeMarco sighed and shook her head. "This does *not* leave this den, Kate. But yes…he told me to keep an eye on you. He actually asked me before we even met for this case."

"What the hell for?"

"He didn't give a reason. I assumed it was because he's getting pressure from the higher-ups about his arrangement with you. He's really pissed that there's a third victim and we haven't made any progress."

"I'm not too thrilled with it, either," Kate said. She was furious—at first. But then she thought she understood it. Had she really been so full of herself to think that as she reached fifty-six years of age she'd be allowed to run violent cases with the same flair as a much younger agent? Of course Duran would have his concerns. The part of it all that pissed her off was that he had not come to her with these worries, but had instead asked her partner to essentially keep tabs on her.

"I'm sorry," DeMarco said. "I told him up front that I was against it."

"It is what it is."

"Kate ... what do you want to do about it? How do we go forward?"

Already heading for the door, Kate responded over her shoulder: "By getting out there and finding a fucking killer."

CHAPTER ELEVEN

In the car, the silence between them was tense—so tense that DeMarco stayed busy with phone calls while Kate drove back into Frankfield. Kate listened to each conversation, staying informed without having to ask questions after each call.

The first call was to the coroner's office. Even while the coroner had stated she would call as soon as they had an accurate guess in regards to a murder weapon, DeMarco called the office to make an official request. She then called the hospital and after being placed on hold for quite a while, got nothing new.

"The doctors say he was only admitted about eight minutes ago and it's too early to tell his condition, though he seems to be alert and in much less pain," DeMarco said. "Once he passes a few stress tests, they'll let us know when he is okay to talk. It could be an hour from now, it could be tomorrow."

"We don't have that long."

It was an obvious statement, one that was driven by Kate's sudden need to not only solve the case, but to make Duran regret ever questioning her abilities. Still, she was also aware that they had no one to question, no leads to follow up on. Right now, it seemed the only avenue they had while waiting for permission to speak to the husband was to continue going over the case notes and revisiting the scene of the murders.

And she had been working this job long enough to know that when that was your only course of action, the case was truly starting to get away from you.

But all she felt was anger and frustration as they closed in on Frankfield—emotions that, when given full control, were also a sure sign that a case was getting the better of her.

Her anger and frustration only heightened when they arrived back at the Frankfield police station. They'd been there four hours ago, reading over the reports and trying to find a thread and now, in that short amount of time, news crews had started to gather. On the far side of the parking lot, Kate saw several cars parked in such a way to block that end of the lot. There were several people milling around in that blocked corner, including a few reporters who were trying to angle in to see what was going on.

"What the hell?" Kate said.

"Is there any way they already found out about the third victim?" DeMarco wondered out loud.

Kate wouldn't be surprised, but the news would have had to travel fast. Other than herself, and DeMarco, Bannerman, the husband, and the coroner, she wasn't sure who else might know. She did know, though, that officers were sometimes paid by local reporters and television news producers to leak information. In a town like Frankfield, not too small in its own right but overshadowed by Chicago, she assumed such a thing was pretty common.

As they pulled into the parking lot, Kate noted a police car on the road just behind them. As it neared the parking lot, the car's bubble lights came on and the driver started to hit the siren in short bursts.

"Must be Bannerman," Kate said as she pulled to the side of the station in search of a parking spot that the media circus had not already grabbed up.

"You been a part of this sort of mess before?" DeMarco asked.

"Far too many times," she said. "They're like sharks in the water, smelling blood. If they know about all three murders, this is going to be very bad."

They stepped out of the car and made their way slowly to the gathered crowd on the opposite corner of the lot. As they approached, Kate noticed another thing that was never good news: someone had set a podium up just adjacent to the station's front doors. Several microphones had been attached to it and three reporters were already standing there, waiting for their moment.

The police car that had come in behind them with the siren bleeping and the lights flashing had stopped in the center of the parking lot, blocking an aisle. The door opened quickly and, sure enough, it was Bannerman who got out. He stormed across the lot toward the gathered crowd in the corner, moving faster than Kate had seen him move since they'd met him. He was yelling something but not in pure anger, merely to be heard over the numerous murmurs in the small crowd.

Kate could hear just enough to grasp what was going on and as she listened, she grew more and more certain that everything that followed was going to be a nightmare.

"Mayor Jennings, you can't just give in to this pressure!"

In the midst of the crowd, a well-dressed woman of about fifty or sixty spoke up. When she spoke, the majority of others around her stopped talking. The reporters, especially, swarmed her like moths to a porch light.

"Sheriff Bannerman, this is not *pressure*. I'd simply like to keep the public informed."

"What good will it do?" Bannerman asked. "Cause panic? Create a few paranoid and hateful Facebook conversations?"

"Perhaps," Mayor Jennings answered. "But maybe it will also light a fire under the collective backsides of you and your officers to do something about a man who has apparently killed three women!"

Ooh, she knows what she's doing, Kate thought. *She's not even at the podium yet and she's giving these reporters exactly what they want.*

With that comment in the air and being devoured by the reporters and cameramen, Mayor Jennings ignored Bannerman completely and made her way to the front of the station where her podium awaited. The reporters and cameramen who weren't already there marched along right behind her. Kate knew they were only doing their jobs, but the news media had always irritated her to no end. Sometimes, in cases like this, she viewed them as no better than the shameless paparazzi that were always chasing after celebrities.

There was half a minute or so of adjustments to mics and the mayor's assistant adjusting her collar and fixing her hair for her. It was all done quickly, as if they all knew that every second was precious—also that they knew if they worked quickly, it would be primed and ready to go for those little news briefs that typically hit the air between noon and one in the afternoon.

As the seemingly random press conference went live, Kate watched Bannerman nestle in along the front row of reporters. He looked nervous and out of place, surely expecting to be called up to speak to the public at some point.

"Ladies and gentlemen," Mayor Jennings said, "I come to you today with some rather unfortunate news. Just over week ago, one of our local Frankfield residents was murdered in her home. The murderer left behind not a single shred of evidence and left our local law enforcement baffled. That, of course, is bad enough, but a second murder occurred just four days ago. It appears that the same killer was responsible for this murder, though we cannot be sure because local law enforcement was not able to come up with any clues, leads, or even any general theories on that case either."

The gathered crowd murmured a bit while also trying to remain professional. There were a few camera snaps, mostly from the automated noise of cell phone cameras. The mayor paused, allowing the moment like a seasoned pro, and then went on. Kate looked over to Bannerman and saw that he looked like he might try to dig a hole and hide at any moment. The anger he'd showed less than three minutes ago had dissolved into absolute helplessness.

It made Kate angry—anger that was merely heaped on the portions of frustration and anger she had been dealing with over the last two days. She was aware that she was clenching her fists, glaring up in anger at a woman she did not even know.

"Then, a little less than three hours ago, another woman was discovered murdered in her own home. And perhaps you already know where I am headed, as it seems to be a trend, but there are no leads or clues coming from the sheriff or his band of local law enforcement. I come to you not to merely inform you of this horrible matter, but to make sure we all take the necessary precautions. All we know at the present moment is that three women are dead—murders that have occurred in the span of about eleven days—and local law enforcement have no leads at the time."

She paused here for dramatic effect, letting that last bit sink in. Here she was, the noble protector, making sure her citizens were informed, while throwing Bannerman under the bus.

"Now," Jennings said, her face sour and bent into an expression of sorrow, "I'd like Sheriff Bannerman to come up to answer any questions you might have."

Kate had seen this before—twice personally in her career and far too many times on the news over the last two decades or so. The mayor had set him up to fail; she'd given him no notice that she was holding the conference, inviting him up to essentially be a blundering mess that would stoke the fires farther.

Bannerman took a hesitant step toward the podium, and that was all Kate could take. She moved quickly, walking to the podium. She saw a man in a dress shirt and jeans moving toward her—perhaps the mayor's security—but she flashed her badge at him. The man looked confused as she stepped up behind the podium. The mayor looked confused, the would-be guard looked confused, and Bannerman looked stunned—and afraid.

A murmur of confusion tore through the crowd as Kate oriented herself. She'd handled press conferences before, but she'd been *invited*. Given that she had barged up to the podium in this one, she knew she had to be firm but not show much emotion. She took a deep breath and did her best to defend Bannerman while also remaining professional.

Almost right away, she felt that she might very well fail.

"Thank you, Mayor Jennings, for the update. As I'm sure you and the gathered media would agree, Sheriff Bannerman's time could be better utilized elsewhere. My name is Agent Kate Wise, here in Frankfield on assignment with the FBI. I can confirm that we currently do not have many leads, but that we are working diligently to find the killer. We do have a few avenues to pursue, but none of it at the level of being public knowledge just yet. As I'm sure you all can understand—perhaps even your esteemed mayor—finding any sort of connections to clues to a death within three hours, as was the case with this morning's victim, is unheard of.

"I have been working with Sheriff Bannerman for the past two days and have seen nothing but seasoned professionalism, hospitality, and a desire to keep his town safe. I recommend we allow him and his force to do their jobs rather than get pinned down by press conferences that are planned at the last minute and with little preparation."

One reporter took advantage of the silence that fell over the crowd after Kate's comments. "What can you tell us about the victims? Are there any connections?"

"I can tell you nothing at the moment—only that your sheriff is working hard to help us find the killer. Thank you."

There was a flurry of questions as Kate left the podium and headed inside.

"How much longer will this maniac be on the streets?"

"How are we supposed to feel safe now?"

"Have any suspects been arrested yet?"

She looked to the mayor and was rather satisfied to see a dumbfounded look on her face. Bannerman fell in beside her with DeMarco trailing behind. DeMarco looked uncertain and, if Kate was reading her correctly, maybe even a little embarrassed.

When the doors closed behind them, Bannerman turned to her right away. He looked baffled, but there was also a thin smile on his face.

"Thank you for that," he said. "There's a whole story there. She's been on my ass ever since she was elected. Her brother ran for sheriff twice and I beat him both times. Petty, sure … but that's how it goes."

"Don't mention it. Of course, I just put my ass on the line. We have to buckle down and find this guy."

DeMarco spoke up, seeming hesitant at first but gaining confidence with each word. "Agent Wise, I'm not so sure this was the smartest thing to do, given our current situation."

"I'm sure it wasn't. But if we let the mayor and the media walk all over this, it makes our work so much harder."

DeMarco nodded and looked away. Kate knew what she was thinking but electing not to say in front of Bannerman: given her current standing with Duran, the move she'd just made at that press conference could have damaged what little bit of trust and respect she still had with Duran. Sooner rather than later, he'd have to cave to the pressure over his head to cut her loose and stop this little experiment.

She was about to ask DeMarco if they could speak in private but didn't get the chance. Bannerman's phone rang and when it did, they all jumped. They also all looked at the phone, hoping it was a break of some kind but not exactly sure what to expect.

"This is Bannerman," he said, answering the call.

Kate and DeMarco waited as Bannerman turned his back to them, listening to the person on the other end. He nodded slowly at first but then a bit faster. After less than twenty seconds, he gave a quick "Thanks," and ended the call.

When he turned back to them, his face was a bit brighter—hopeful, even. "That was one of the nurses tending to David Lowell, Meredith's wife. He's looking okay for now but the docs are still not allowing us to talk to him. However, David told them to let us know that there's a Nest security camera outside the house … hiding behind an azalea bush in the flower bed in the front yard. The doctors have allowed him to log into his security account on a laptop at the hospital to give us access to the footage. The security company just has to verify it … and that could take a while."

"Not after I make a call to them, it won't," DeMarco said. "You got the name of the security company?"

Bannerman gave it to her and with a quick Google search on her phone she was speaking to a representative for the company in less than two minutes. Kate, DeMarco, and Bannerman filed into his office once again as DeMarco spoke to the representative, hopefully nailing down the corners to not only their first solid lead, but footage that would nab them a killer by the end of the day.

CHAPTER TWELVE

DeMarco did indeed have a knack for working her way around a conversation. Without being too rude but applying just the right amount of urgency and force, she had a tech specialist with the company helping to patch the footage through to one of the precinct's laptops. Less than fifteen minutes after making the call, they had a remote version of the Lowells' security log-in screen on the laptop. The specialist helped them through it, explained how the system worked, and then directed them to that morning's security footage.

The camera was different than the one at the Hixes' residence, as it was constantly on. The footage for the day started at 12:01 a.m. With the technician's help, they were able to fast forward through the footage until the first movement of the day could be seen on the screen.

"Right there, stop," Kate said.

The technician, on speaker mode through DeMarco's cell phone, responded right away. "Got it. Right there …."

Kate, DeMarco, and Bannerman watched the screen as a man came out of the house at 8:12. Having never seen David Lowell, Kate turned to Bannerman for verification. "Did you see the husband before he was placed in the ambulance?"

"Yeah, that's him."

"Okay," Kate spoke up, making sure the technician heard her. "You can skip ahead."

They watched as the tech took over the screen again and skipped the footage ahead. After a few minutes (which equated to nearly an hour on the fast-forwarded footage), a shape appeared in the left-hand side of the screen, just before the screen went black. In fast-forward mode, the blackness was just a blip on the radar, but it was enough for the tech to stop the footage.

"What happened?" DeMarco asked.

"The feed was cut."

"Any idea how?"

"Not just yet, but I can check the records to see. But honestly, to me, it looks like a manual termination. When the cameras have some sort of failure or malfunction, there is typically a little white flash before the screen goes black. I can check those records right now."

"Before you do, can you backtrack the footage to ten seconds before it went out?" Kate asked.

"Sure thing."

The footage went backward, showing that same angle of sidewalk, yard, and stilted sky beyond. When the tech stopped and the playback was in regular speed, they all watched the left side of the screen. In actual speed, the shape that came into view was much more than just a shape: it was a figure.

A man. He was wearing what looked to be some sort of uniform—a navy-blue uniform with some sort of logo on the left breast. His face wasn't completely in the shot, but there was enough to make out several features; he appeared to be a younger man with scruff on his face that could not quite be called a beard. He was walking quickly toward the porch, but he was in the shot for no more than a second and a half before the screen went black.

"Can we see that last three seconds again?" Kate asked. "And when it gets to that man, can you freeze it?"

"Absolutely."

The tech did as asked and five seconds later, they were looking at a still-frame image of the man. Kate was irritated that the angle of the camera did not show his entire face but there was enough there.

"Thanks," Kate said.

"Of course. Give me a few seconds and I can maybe tell you why the screen went out."

While the tech put them on hold, Kate, DeMarco, and Bannerman studied the picture of the man. Kate stared at the uniform. It looked like the sort most UPS drivers wore but the logo on the shirt was definitely not UPS. It made her think of Mike Wallace and his Hexco uniform. This uniform was a bit more casual, though. The pants looked to be just dark jeans, the navy button-down shirt tucked into it.

"Sheriff Bannerman, do you have any idea what that uniform might be?"

Bannerman, already leaning in close, leaned in a bit more. "No, I don't think so. If I could see that logo on the breast pocket of his shirt…"

Apparently, the tech had overheard this. "I can do that for you," she said proudly.

They watched as she took control of the screen again, blew the image up, and positioned the logo on the shirt in the center of the screen.

"Ah," Bannerman said. "That's a driver for Panther Shipping."

"What's that?" Kate asked.

"A small shipping company that has its HQ in Chicago but delivers all over most of the state. They're bigger in the cities and towns within an hour or so of Chicago. Sort of a local and more secure method for shipping. A lot of local companies use them for heavier equipment. We used them just a few months ago when they were delivering some of the steel rods and columns for the new bunker we have for the patrol cars out back."

"So I wonder what they were delivering," Kate wondered out loud.

"Where are we on figuring out how the feed was killed?" Bannerman asked the tech.

The tech sounded confused when she started speaking but by the time she had given the entire answer, she sounded as if she knew what had been going on.

"I see right here that someone logged into the system on a mobile device to deactivate the camera. It was done on a device from within the house."

"And it was never turned back on?" Kate asked.

"No ma'am."

"Thank you so much for your help."

"Of course. Call us back if you need any further assistance."

With the tech off of the phone, the three looked at one another, a disappointed sort of grin spreading across DeMarco's face. "Well," she said, "at least we know what he was delivering."

It was a poor joke, but Kate assumed she was right. Meredith Lowell had killed the feed, hoping to hide the fact that this man had visited. Apparently, she had not cut it off soon enough, though, granting them this brief shot of her visitor.

And seeing as how Meredith had never gotten the chance to turn the Nest camera back on, it was very likely that the man still centered on the laptop screen was the killer.

"Can you print this picture out for me?" Kate asked, getting to her feet. "I'd like to have it in my possession when I pay a visit to Panther Shipping."

The Panther Shipping delivery depot was located just outside of Chicago's city limits. It was a respectable building, with a large office with glass-paneled walls on the right, connected to eight loading bays to the left. Two of the bays were occupied when Kate and DeMarco arrived. A large paved lot that surrounded the right side of the building currently housed eleven trucks; multiple empty parking spaces on that end indicated that Panther possessed at least fifteen more trucks. Most of the ones in the lot were larger delivery vans, though there were two eighteen-wheelers with trailers behind them.

Inside, the place was decked out in all sorts of pictures of drivers and awards hanging in the central office. They walked to the reception window, where an older lady greeted them with a smile.

"Can I help you ladies?" she asked.

"Yes, please," Kate said. She politely slid her badge and ID across the counter and said, "We have a picture of one of your drivers that was taken with a security camera at a private residence this morning. We'd like to have the man IDed—by a manager if there is one on duty."

The older woman looked alarmed but nodded and wasted no time. She reached instantly for the phone on her desk. "Of course! Just one moment."

She turned away and started speaking to someone on the other end in a hushed tone. Less than thirty seconds later, she turned back to them. Her smile was gone now, her face all business. "Mr. Morris is coming out right this moment," she said.

"Thank you."

Apparently, the people at Panther Shipping took these things very seriously; Kate and DeMarco had not even had a proper moment to sit down before a man dressed in a button-down shirt and khakis came from around the corner. A bit of a beer belly hung over his belted waist and he looked cautiously at them through thin reading glasses.

He got closer to them before he asked: "Are you the agents?"

"We are," DeMarco said.

"My name is Henry Morris, the regional manager. Please come with me to my office," he said. He was basically pleasing, hoping they could cover this in private, without an easy-to-overhear conversation or without anyone pulling out IDs or badges.

"Lead the way," Kate said.

Relief washed over his face as he led them out of the central office and down an attached hallway. More pictures of drivers, trucks, and hanging awards lined the hallways. The office Morris led them into was of a modest size but quite tidy. A large whiteboard hung on the right wall, lined with what looked like delivery schedules, times, and the names of several drivers.

Kate respected the fact that after he closed the door, Morris did not sit down behind the desk. He stayed on his feet, standing by the whiteboard. He looked nervous, making Kate assume he had never had many dealings with the law.

"Pamela tells me you had a question about one of our drivers?" he said.

"We do," Kate said. She reached into her inside jacket pocket and removed the picture that Bannerman had printed out for them. "We need to know who this man is."

Morris looked at it for just a moment before he answered. "That's Ashley Watts. He's been a driver with us for about two years now. Has he done something wrong?"

"It looks like he might have," Kate said. "And for his own interests as well as those of your company, I'd like to speak with him before I give you any details. Is he still on delivery?"

Morris glanced at his watch and shook his head. "No. He should have come back about an hour or so ago. He's still here, though. He's one of our backup drivers for any deliveries that come in late."

"Could you get him in here, please?"

"I can indeed," he said. It was then that he finally sat down behind his desk. He picked up the receiver on the phone, punched in two numbers to page a department, and then said: "Hey, thanks. Could you send Ashley to my office? And quickly, please."

When he hung up, he looked up at Kate and DeMarco with that same worry on his face. "I do hope there's nothing serious here. We've been in business for over ten years now and the most trouble our drivers have ever been in were speeding tickets—and there have only been four total."

"Hopefully it will remain that way when we leave here," Kate said. But she thought of seeing the man on the Nest feed—a man they now knew as being named Ashley Watts—and didn't think that would be the case.

The three of them remained in silence until there was a knock on the door about a minute and a half later.

"Come on in," Morris said.

The man who entered was unmistakably the man from Meredith Lowell's Nest camera feed. When he came into the office, he even presented the same side of his face that had been seen on the frozen picture. He looked around the office, clearly perplexed at seeing the two women, and started to close the door behind him.

"Actually, Mr. Morris," DeMarco said, "would you mind giving us your office for a few minutes?"

"Absolutely," he said. When he walked toward the door he still looked worried, but very happy that he was given permission to leave. When he closed the door behind him, he did so quietly, as if he were trying his best not to disturb them.

"You're Ashley Watts, correct?" Kate asked.

"I am. And you are?"

He had an air of confidence about him that Kate could tell he was doing his best to keep in check. She watched it falter significantly as she showed him her ID. "I'm Agent Wise and this is Agent DeMarco, with the FBI. We have some questions about your morning deliveries."

Watts instantly turned red in the face. He shifted uncomfortably from foot to foot and nodded slowly. Kate knew the look, as she had seen it numerous times in the past. It was the look of someone who had been busted and was trying to decide if they should just accept it or try to worm their way out of it.

"Looks like you might know what we're talking about already," DeMarco said. "Want to go ahead and tell us why you think we're here?"

Still red in the face, Watts looked at them skeptically. He reminded Kate of a kid who visited the principal, unsure if he was there to be awarded or punished. "Well, I can maybe think of something some might view as bad, but I certainly don't think it would warrant a visit from the FBI."

Kate handed him the same picture she had handed Henry Morris just a few moments ago. Watts looked confused at first but then realization started to sink into his features.

"This from the security camera at the Lowell house?" he asked.

"It is," Kate answered. "Does that not surprise you?"

"I don't know. Meredith…she's supposed to cut the feed off when I come over."

"So you've been by there before…for non-delivery purposes?"

"I have. But…still. I get that affairs are bad. But why is the FBI involved?"

"Because," Kate said, "sometime in the three and a half hours between her husband leaving for work and arriving back home just before noon, Meredith Lowell was killed."

She could have kept going but decided to stop there; she wanted to catch his reaction to that bombshell of news. He started to grin, as though thinking it was some sort of a joke, but then his face went absolutely blank. He blinked a few times, then said one simple word.

"What?"

"She was murdered this morning, and this picture of you entering her home is the last thing the Nest camera captured."

"Well, but…yeah…but…" He stopped here, his expression growing grave as he started to realize what was being insinuated. When he started speaking again, it was clear that he was having to focus on each and every word. "We'd hooked up at least a dozen times. She told me she'd always kill the feed on that thing if I was coming over…said her husband never checked it anyway. I don't know if maybe she forgot or what this time…"

"How long were you in her home this morning?" Kate asked.

"I don't know. It um…well, it was never really for very long. When we were done, she wasn't one for wanting me to hang around. She's married, you know? She wanted me out of there as soon as possible."

"So sex, clean up, and leave?" DeMarco asked.

"Basically. Sometimes we wouldn't even make it to the bed or the couch. A few times it was right there in the foyer, against the wall or the door."

"And what about this morning?" Kate asked.

"In the den. On the couch."

"How long?"

"I don't know. Maybe fifteen or twenty minutes."

"So let's say that's accurate," Kate said. "Then why did she not turn the security camera back on after you left?"

"I don't know. Maybe she forgot. She…I mean…*shit!* She's really dead?"

"She is," Kate said. "And so far as we know, you're the last person she saw. You understand why that makes you a suspect, right?"

"I guess, but…but that's insane."

"Do you have proof that you didn't hang around longer than those few minutes?"

"I can show you all of the timestamps on the packages I delivered after that. Hell, there was one house just up the street from her."

"How can you show us?"

"I can use my scanner to show you. It's back in my locker, if you'll let me go get it."

"That's fine," Kate said. "Of course, you understand if we accompany you?"

"Yeah, that's fine."

Kate wasn't sure, but she thought she saw what looked like the beginnings of tears forming in the corners of his eyes. This did nothing to sway her. And honestly, even if Watts's scanner showed that he had been scanning packages within half an hour of David Lowell leaving for work, it would not clear Watts in her mind. He could have had sex with her, killed her, and then left the house all in the space of five minutes. It was possible.

Besides…there was her intuition to consider. And one of the hard to believe things she had come to accept about sexual relationships was that when there were affairs, it was *incredibly* rare for a male lover to kill the woman; almost ninety percent of the time, it was the husband.

As Watts led them to the back of the building and then to the left toward the loading bay, they passed by a pacing Mr. Morris, gripping a cup of coffee as if it were a life preserver. He looked worried, very concerned about the state of his driver and his company.

And honestly, Kate didn't blame him. The media was already all over these murders. If they caught wind that a Panther Shipping driver was in any way involved—even if it was just an affair with one of the victims—it would be terrible for business.

She could sympathize…because if she didn't wrap this case soon, it could be equally terrible for her career and the reputation she had spent thirty years building.

Kate and DeMarco sat in the small break room just outside of the loading bays of Panther Shipping. Through the large window that looked out into the large adjoined loading area, they could see Morris and Watts speaking. They were huddled closely together, giving wary glances to anyone who happened to pass by.

Kate was looking at the printout Watts had handed them after coming straight from his scanner. It looked like a very thin grocery store receipt, showing all of the stops Watts had made that morning. There was, of course, no listed stop for the Lowell residence, but there was one several houses up, punched in exactly nineteen minutes after Meredith Lowell had cut off the security camera at her house. The list was forty-six stops long—five of which had come before his stop by the Lowell residence.

"I don't see how this proves anything," DeMarco said. "Nineteen minutes is more than enough time to have sex and then strangle someone."

"I agree with that part," Kate said, "but I still don't think Ashley Watts is the killer."

"Care to explain?"

"Well, he said they've hooked up several times before. A simple look back through the Lowells' Nest footage can confirm that—even if only to show that it was turned off before he arrived. So I doubt he's lying about the affair. And from my experience, it is *rarely* the lover that kills the married party in an affair; it's usually the jilted spouse."

DeMarco nodded as she looked at the printout. Kate assumed she had learned the same thing somewhere along the way during her time in the academy. "Still…he strikes me as a fit. I want to check his truck and his locker."

"I won't stop you."

DeMarco got to her feet and left the break room. Kate trailed behind, fairly certain that Watts was not their man, but wanting to give DeMarco her own space to run with her instincts. As they approached Morris and Watts, Kate let DeMarco handle the conversation. She would be supportive but didn't see the point in piling on.

"Mr. Watts," DeMarco said, "I'd like to see inside your truck, please."

Watts looks at Morris and gave a nervous little shrug. "I'm fine with it."

"That's fine," Morris agreed.

"It's parked in spot eleven out in the lot," Watts said.

"What have you taken out of it that would have been in it when you stopped by the Lowell residence?"

"My lunchbox and my backpack. Those are both in my locker."

"I'd like to have a look in the locker as well. Your backpack and lunchbox, too."

"Sure," Watts said, already digging into his pocket. He took out a small key ring and handed it over without hesitation. "The bigger one is to the truck. The one with the little yellow head is to my locker." He pointed behind them to the row of orange lockers bolted into the wall. "Mine is number twenty."

DeMarco started over toward the locker, Kate still letting her take the lead. With each bit of permission Watts gave, Kate became more and more sure that he was innocent. She could tell by the slight slouch in DeMarco's posture that she was becoming a bit more convinced of Watts's innocence as well.

Still, Kate did her best to remain a loyal partner. When DeMarco took Watts's backpack and lunchbox from his locker, Kate helped her search. It did not take long, as the lunchbox was empty with the exception of a small empty bag of Doritos, and the backpack only contained his wallet, a Lee Child paperback, and a change of clothes.

Kate noted that Watts was watching it all. He still looked rather distraught but there was a sense of calm about him now. If anything, she thought he looked genuinely confused that two FBI agents were going to such great lengths to search his possessions.

Without saying a word, DeMarco returned the pack and lunch-box to Watts's locker and headed straight to one of the loading bay doors, where the parking lot waited outside. She walked to parking spot eleven and to the truck positioned there. She used the key to unlock the double doors on the back, swung them open, and stepped inside. Kate followed behind, surprised to find that there was still a small part of her that hoped they might find something.

The back of the truck contained only a few straps and carabiner clips hanging from the walls. There was scattered detritus here and there—a partially broken board that was scarred up in a way to indicate it was often used to pry larger boxes away from the walls of the truck. The only thing suspicious in the truck was a length of nylon rope, bundled up neatly. DeMarco picked it up and examined it. She showed it to Kate, shrugging as Kate took it from her.

"It could easily be used as a means of strangulation," Kate said. "But I think it might be too thick. The nylon could certainly cause some of the abrasions we're seeing, but you have to remember that with Karen Hopkins, whatever was used to strangle her was so thin that it slightly cut into her skin. The only way you're going to get this nylon rope to do that is if you're yanking it back and forth—and if that were the case, there would be more of a rope burn look to the area."

"I thought so, too," DeMarco said. She took the rope back and tossed it down. "Shit. I was sure it was him."

"I was hoping it was, too," Kate said. It dawned on her then that this was not the first time she had witnessed DeMarco pushing hard to pin down a suspect who had been involved in an affair with a married murder victim. She wondered if there might be something in her partner's past that caused this.

"Well, even if it's not him, it's obvious he knows at least a thing or two about Meredith Lowell," DeMarco pointed out. "So he might not be a suspect, but he'd certainly be a potential source of information."

Almost comically, DeMarco sat down on the floor of the back of the truck. "This one is getting to me, Kate."

"If it didn't, I'd question your heart."

"No, I mean…all cases get to me in a certain way. But this one…this one is really screwing me up. And I don't know why."

"It's a common feeling. And I know it sounds all go-get-'em and whatnot, but the best way to find out why a case is having such an effect on you is to wrap it. Typically, once the killer is apprehended and the smaller details of the case start to fall in place, you'll be able to step back and see it from a bit of a distance."

"You talk like you've experienced it before."

"More times than I can count."

"Guys like this…guys like Watts…they piss me off. My own parents were both involved in affairs. And they forgave one another…gave it another try, you know? And it fucking crashed and burned after that."

Kate did not take the time to feel affirmation from having called it less than a minute ago. Instead, she reached down and offered a hand to help DeMarco back to her feet. "Family demons can make it even harder to figure out why a case is getting away from you," Kate said. "And to be honest with you, I'm dealing with that very same thing right now."

"So how are you able to deal with it so well?"

"Because I'm allowing things to fall apart back home."

The answer was out of her mouth before she was aware she was going to say it. And though it felt freeing, there was some sting there as well. DeMarco seemed taken aback at the honesty of it, too. She took Kate's offered hand and got back to her feet. Before starting back for the opened doors at the back of Watts's truck, she smirked and said: "So let's wrap this. Let's get that distance."

Returning the snarky little grin, Kate nodded. "Sure. Just lead the way."

CHAPTER THIRTEEN

Kate and DeMarco had dinner delivered to the Frankfield precinct, filling the building's one conference room with the smell of Chinese food. Bannerman was sitting at one end of the table, slowly chewing on the egg roll Kate had offered him. Bannerman and Kate were looking up at the dry erase board as DeMarco stood by it, jotting down notes underneath pictures they had attached to the board with magnets. The pictures came from each of the three crime scenes, the ones from the Lowell residence fresh from the printer. DeMarco jotted the notes down for each case, connecting what seemed like common links with little broken dash marks that stretched across the entirety of the board. Sadly, there were very few of these.

So far, they had come up with the fact that the Hopkinses had not had a security system of any kind in place, making Karen Hopkins unique in those aspects. Then there was the fact that the Hix residence had been the only site that had a secondary entrance, allowing the killer to sidestep a security camera altogether. There had been the connection that the women were middle-aged wives with non-responsive husbands, but that theory had been dashed with Meredith Lowell; sure, she had been involved in an affair but her husband seemed to have basically arranged his world around her.

And while there *were* still obvious connections, none of them led anywhere. All of them were at home by themselves during the day. They had all been strangled by someone they had apparently willingly allowed into their homes.

But the two most important questions remained, and they were on the board in DeMarco's handwriting, circled in red: *Who? Why?*

"This makes no sense," Bannerman said. "Either the killer knew that Meredith Lowell was having an affair and exactly when Watts was coming by, or it was sheer luck."

"Or," Kate said, "he had been scheduled to come by. Maybe Meredith told the killer an exact time to come by the house. After all, it appears she allowed him in."

"And Watts already told us when we left Panther Shipping that she never mentioned anyone coming by," DeMarco said.

"That means nothing," Kate said. "As we have discovered, she was apparently very good at keeping secrets."

"Well," Bannerman said, "I've got several officers reaching out to family and friends of the victims, looking for any sort of a connection between them. Even right down to the minute details like which gyms they belonged to and their pizza place of choice. We're looking for anything—grasping at any straw available."

"Sometimes that can be more helpful than you realize," Kate said.

Just as the comment was out of her mouth, her phone rang from inside her jacket pocket. She grabbed it, saw that it was Director Duran, and got to her feet. "Sorry," she said. "I have to take this."

As she stepped outside of the conference room, she did her best to calm her nerves. She wanted to ask him right away why he felt that DeMarco needed to babysit her. She wanted to ask him if the career she had built for herself meant nothing to him. But she knew she could not let her temper get the better of her. After all, she and Duran had been working together in come capacity or another for nearly twenty years. She respected him and trusted him implicitly. If he had DeMarco checking on her, surely there was a reason.

But he was calling her now, not DeMarco. Perhaps it was to even apologize or to give her some sort of encouragement.

Kate answered on the fourth ring. "This is Wise."

"Kate, I need you to explain what was going on in your mind when you decided to storm in front of the cameras at a press conference."

"And hello to you, too."

"Kate, this is no time to be funny. We've worked together for twenty-one years and I don't think I've ever been this enraged at you."

"Well, did you see the entire thing?"

"I did," Duran said. "And I know what you were doing. You were trying to help out an older sheriff who was clearly being bullied by an asshole of a mayor. But still…by getting in front of those cameras, you basically made yourself the face of this case—a case, I might add, that now has three victims and not a single lead."

"If I'd had time to think it through, I might not have done it," Kate admitted. "But as you saw, that conference was thrown together hastily…probably for nothing more than to take a swing at local law enforcement. But I did not have time and I acted on instinct. And for that, I'm sorry."

"Has there been any progress on the case since that little blunder?"

"Not really. We found a guy who was having an affair with the latest victim, but he's got some pretty tight alibis. He's agreed to stay in the area for repeated questioning if necessary."

"And that's all?"

Kate felt her own little flash of rage stirring inside of her. "We're in a conference room with Sheriff Bannerman right now, trying to find a common thread."

"Three victims, Kate. Working in a conference room isn't enough. Look…I really hate to do this but after the stunt with the press conference and an absolute lack of leads, I have no real choice. I'm going to have to pull you off the case."

"Excuse me?" Some of the rage came through in these two words and as juvenile as it made her feel, it still felt incredibly good.

"You know how this works, Kate. An agent has been on public television, speaking about a case. In this case, that just happens to be you. Not only is there huge pressure coming from farther up the ladder all dumped on me, but the media is all over it and so far you and DeMarco have absolutely nothing to show."

"And you think it's going to look better for you to pull the face that you yourself said you believe is now representative of the case?"

"It's better than nothing. It will show the public that we are actively on the case and that we keep tight reins on our agents."

"So you just want us to come in and leave the case to some other pair?" Kate asked, incredulous.

"I'm afraid you didn't hear me right. I just want *you* off. I have another agent assigned to work with DeMarco."

"Are you kidding me right now?"

"I'm afraid not. Look…it's late in the evening. Get some rest and head back in the morning."

"Duran, you can't possibly—"

"Be smart about this, Kate. Know when to stop talking. I expect to see you in my office for debrief no later than ten o'clock tomorrow morning."

Even if she could have thought of something logical to say, she did not have the chance. Duran ended the call before she could even wrap her mind around what had just happened. She stared at the phone, deeply confused and angry, before slowly walking back into the conference room.

DeMarco was writing down the few details they had on Ashley Watts while Bannerman was polishing off the egg roll. Kate looked at the whiteboard and realized that Duran was right: they had nothing, seemed to be going absolutely nowhere, and maybe it *had* been irresponsible of her to jump in front of the cameras like that.

The whiteboard told the story. No clues, no connection. Theories that were being blown apart with each victim.

Maybe you're getting too old for this.

The thought came out of nowhere and was like a dagger to the heart. It hurt even worse, like that dagger being twisted, when she imagined a younger agent working alongside DeMarco.

"Everything okay?" DeMarco asked, looking away from the board to grab a large forkful of orange chicken.

"Yeah," she lied. She took her seat and stared up at the absolute lack of answers on the whiteboard in front of her. "Where were we?"

❧ ❧ ❧

When she and DeMarco drove back to the hotel at 8:35, Kate nearly told DeMarco about the call Duran had placed. In the end, she decided not to. She assumed Duran had also called DeMarco to fill her in and, if that were the case, DeMarco had not mentioned it and was choosing to keep it to herself. Kate wondered if DeMarco was trying to protect her or if she found the situation too awkward to handle. Or maybe Duran *hadn't* called DeMarco at all. Maybe he was waiting to see how she would handle it—if she would totally blow up at him or if she'd be the good little agent and come back home for her punishment without putting up a fight.

DeMarco parked the car and got out, apparently noting how quiet Kate had been for the past several hours.

"You going to tell me what's wrong?" she asked.

"I'd really rather not."

"Fair enough. Want to have a few drinks and then *accidentally* tell me?"

Kate shook her head. "At the risk of seeming like a bitch, I think I just want to spend some time alone tonight."

They were walking toward their rooms, Kate fumbling with her keys, when DeMarco reached out and took her hand. "Wise… *Kate*… I hope you know I consider you more than my partner. More than a good agent, even. I consider you a friend. That being said, I want you to know that you can tell me anything."

That settles it then, Kate thought. *Duran hasn't called her yet. He's wanting me to tell her.*

Still, she couldn't bring herself to say it. She did not want to admit defeat to this woman who was looking up to her as a mentor of sorts.

"I'm fine," Kate said. "Just tired and bummed out about all of the stuff going on back home with Melissa."

"Okay. I'll leave you to your own stuff tonight. Me, I'll be heading back to the bar. If you change your mind, I'd love to have you."

"Sounds good."

"But if you aren't there within a few hours, maybe stay put. If that same bartender is working tonight, I may embarrass you."

"Embarrass me how?"

DeMarco grinned as they reached their respective rooms, side by side. "Not that you're old-fashioned or stuck up or anything, but you don't strike me as the sort of woman that would be overly comfortable being in the presence of a gay woman trying to pick up another gay woman."

"Thanks... I think. I would *not* be uncomfortable with that, by the way. Also, that gives me one more reason to stay in. You go do your thing. Let me know how it goes in the morning."

"Yeah, I'll do that," DeMarco said.

She looked rather surprised at how well Kate had responded. It again made Kate wonder just how much of an obstacle DeMarco's homosexuality had been as she had come up through high school, college, and even the academy. Kate knew the bureau took great strides to promote inclusion, but some individuals within the academy were still, even to this day, unable to shake racial and sexual biases.

Kate walked into her room, kicked her shoes off, and fell onto the bed like a tired and angst-ridden teen. She let out a huge exhale of air, figuring it was much more mature and productive than screaming into a pillow.

Perhaps it was the uncharacteristic anger that had her so riled up, but she decided in that moment that she was not going to leave the case. She assumed that at some point, Duran could threaten her—perhaps even with being arrested for interfering in a case that was no longer hers—but she didn't think he would do such a thing. She knew Duran well enough to know that he was damned good at being scary and demanding certain things of people, but he was often very slow to pull the trigger when it came to doling out consequences and punishments. Besides, even if he did come down hard on her, what was he going to do? The absolute worst he could do was fire her and while that would certainly be a blow, Kate figured it might be just the exit strategy she needed—a forced one.

As she tried to sort through all of this, her phone rang. She dug it out of her pocket and saw that it was Melissa. She nearly swiped her finger across the screen to answer the call but stopped herself at the last minute. She placed the phone facedown and waited for the buzzing to stop.

Don't tear yourself up, Kate told herself. *She has to learn to deal with things on her own. She has to learn that just because things are better between the two of you, she can't come rushing to you whenever something is bothering her. If there's something related to Michelle and her health, Melissa will leave a message and you can respond. But for now, you have to let her learn to navigate life on her own.*

Kate knew that tears were brimming in her eyes over these thoughts—but she also knew they were true.

It was then, contemplating the meaning behind Melissa's calls, that Kate started to wonder how Alan was doing. He had always been quite good about not calling her when she was on a case, but he would typically text her every now and then when she was away, just to let her know he was thinking about her. Ever since she had left two days ago, leaving him with Michelle, she had not gotten a single text.

And that's fine, she thought. *I'm not sure I want to speak to him after he gave me his little spiel about "getting my priorities straight."*

She lay there for a very long time, staring at the ceiling and trying to remain calm. She'd experienced far too much anger over the last few days—an emotion she typically managed to stay very far away from. It had thrown her off and, if she was being honest with herself, felt toxic.

She wasn't sure how long she had been lying there when she realized just how tired she was. Hadn't she read somewhere that copious amounts of anger tended to tire out those who weren't accustomed to the emotion? She nearly got up from the bed but decided against it. She simply lay still, wallowing in it all, until she fell asleep far earlier than she had intended.

❖ ❖ ❖

While she slept, she dreamed. It was the sort of dream where the dreamer is somehow fully aware it's a dream, but that realization does nothing to stem the impact of it.

In the dream, she was walking into a well-to-do home with DeMarco. The was similar to most of the homes she had been in ever since taking the new position with the bureau after coming out of retirement: well built, trendy, and over-expensive. As she made her way through the home, she came to a man standing over a body in the living room. The body on the floor was that of a woman, her face turned toward Kate in a horrified expression.

It was her daughter ... it was Melissa.

She had been strangled, but with something much harsher than what had killed the three women in Frankfield. Whatever had strangled Melissa had sliced deeply into her throat, her head barely hanging on to her neck.

Unmoved, Kate stepped forward. The man standing over the body turned around and looked at her. It was Terry. He had been weeping so much that the area around his eyes had been rubbed red. The corner of his right eye was torn, trickling little drops of blood.

"She was here alone," Terry said. "I was at work and ... my God, I just didn't show her I loved her enough, did I? I was too distant, too ..."

On the floor, Melissa opened her mouth. Doing so made it appear as if her head would separate from her shoulders completely. She mouthed just two words; they were soundless, but Kate knew what they were.

"Mom ... help ..."

"Terry," Kate said. "What happened?"

"I don't know," he wailed, his eye still bleeding. "I wish I knew. I wish I'd paid more attention to her. I wish ... I wish you knew yourself."

In the dream, Kate only stared at the body of her daughter with the eye of a seasoned agent.

But in a hotel room in Frankfield, Illinois, she moaned in her sleep.

CHAPTER FOURTEEN

When Kate stirred awake just after 5:30 the following morning, the dream was still prevalent in her mind. She saw Terry's bleeding eyes looking at her as if she had the answers, as if she might know why that dream version of Melissa was dead. As haunting as the dream was, it slammed one determined thought to the front of her head. It was an obvious next step in the process, but one that she and DeMarco had been patiently waiting on.

Well, Kate thought as she made her way to the bathroom and brushed her teeth, *patience isn't something I have time for right now. When I'm not back in DC by noon, Duran is going to know I disobeyed him. He'll start calling. And I'll ignore him. I have no idea how long it will be before he calls Bannerman and his men, giving them authority to arrest me.*

She sorted through all of this as she did her best with her hair. She had, after all, fallen asleep without getting properly ready for bed the night before. Her neck hurt and the dream felt as if it had glued itself to the very center of her mind.

No, she did not have time to be patient or by-the-book. She had *maybe* six hours to get something done. And as much as she hated to go rogue on DeMarco, she honestly didn't see that she had much of a choice.

She was going to have to go by the hospital and hope she could get in to see David Lowell. Even if he was not medically cleared yet, she had to figure out some way to speak with him. Over the past thirty years or so, she'd spoken with numerous people in various states of injury—a few even on their deathbeds. She knew when to push and when to pull back. And without DeMarco watching over her shoulder, Kate thought she might be able to get away with flirting with the boundary between the two.

She was fastening her holster, perhaps a minute or two from stepping out the door, when her phone rang. She checked the display and saw that it was Bannerman. She nearly ignored it and headed out on her mission but figured it made no sense to dodge his calls. There was always the chance that he might have information no one else did. When you were the sheriff of a town the size of Frankfield, the breaks in nearly all developing stories went to you first, even when the FBI is in town.

She answered it, almost feeling as if she had been busted. "This is Wise."

"Agent Wise, it's Bannerman. I just got a call from David Lowell. He's home. He apparently got home around midnight last night, about an hour after he was discharged. The hospital didn't bother calling when he was given the okay to speak to us, as I asked them to. But I just got off of the phone with him. Seems he was unable to sleep and wants to talk to us—wants to find out who killed his wife and why."

Now she *really* felt like she had been busted. She was relieved to know that Lowell was back home and more than willing to speak with them, but at the same time, working alongside Bannerman and DeMarco would only slow her down. She gritted her teeth in frustration but carried on as expected.

"That's great, Sheriff. Can you meet us at the hotel in about ten minutes?"

"I'm already on the way."

Kate was impressed at how quickly DeMarco got dressed and ready for the day. She'd still been asleep when Kate knocked on her door at 5:51, answering the door and then leaving it cracked for Kate to walk in while she scrambled around the room to get ready. Kate noted the empty bed and grinned.

"Did you strike out last night?"

"No, I'd call it a home run. I told her what I do for a living and that it wasn't practical for her to sleep here. She agreed and left."

"Good for you," Kate said.

DeMarco smirked as she buttoned up her shirt. "For her, too."

Bannerman arrived just as Kate and DeMarco headed out of the room in hopes that the crappy little hotel office served complimentary coffee.

"No need," Bannerman said as they approached the car. "I figured you'd need some for this early hour and brought you each a cup of the petrol we drink from down at the station. Breakfast, on the other hand…"

"We can wait," DeMarco said, though it sounded like a question as she looked over to Kate.

"Yes," Kate agreed. "We can wait."

Bannerman seemed pleased when they got into his patrol car rather than opting for their own. He sped out of the lot and took the familiar two-lanes through the city until he came to the trendy little subdivision the Lowells had happily lived in until yesterday. Kate frowned when she realized the house already had that feeling she had somehow gotten used to and had come to accept—the feel of a residence that is no longer a happy home but now a place of trauma and sorrow. It was far too similar to pulling up to a funeral parlor.

They made their way up the porch, Kate knocking on the door while DeMarco and Bannerman kept a respectable distance behind as to not make the grieving husband feel too overwhelmed.

The door was answered by a woman of about forty or so. She looked tired but had the air of a woman who was getting things done. She nodded to them all before saying anything.

"FBI?" she asked in a hopeful tone.

"Yes," Kate said. "Agents Wise and DeMarco. This is Sheriff Bannerman," she said, gesturing to Bannerman, "with the local PD."

"I'm Paulette Ivans, David's sister," the woman said. "I've been with him from the moment he was admitted to the hospital. I made the request for the doctors not to call you when he was given the clear. David…I don't know. I don't think it was so much a heart attack as it was a heart *break*. I know that sounds cheesy, but it sums it all up pretty well."

"But he's fine now?" DeMarco asked.

"Fine enough to make it through the details, I think," Paulette said. "He badly wants to talk to you to figure this all out. Just…I wouldn't be at all surprised if he breaks down while you're here. He hasn't really talked deeply about it. If he does have a breakdown, I'd greatly appreciate it if you'd leave. I'll call you back when he is ready."

"Understood," Kate said.

"Come on in, then."

Paulette led them into the Lowell home. Just like the exterior, the interior simply felt gloomy. It was clear that a great deal of grieving was being done; Kate could feel it in the air. Paulette led them to the living room, where David Lowell was sitting in an armchair and looking out the window. He glanced toward them at once when they entered the room and the amount of absolute hope in his eyes slayed Kate.

"Mr. Lowell, I'm Agent Wise and this is Agent DeMarco."

"Yeah, I was told the FBI was in town on this but…I mean, I appreciate it, but *why*?"

"I assume neither of you have seen the news?" Bannerman asked.

"No," Paulette said. "Why?"

Kate stepped forward after giving Bannerman an unsteady glance. "Ms. Ivans, Mr. Lowell…this was the third murder of this kind here in Frankfield over the past two weeks or so."

"Oh," he said. He went wide-eyed for a moment, as if he was awed by this information, but it did not last long. "Are there any suspects so far?"

"I'm afraid not," Kate said. "None that have panned out, anyway. We were hoping you might have some ideas."

"Not a single one. I've been trying to figure it out ever since I was coherent enough to do so. It just doesn't make sense. I can't think of anyone that had anything against her. It had to be some random asshole, preying on random women. I called the security company because when I tried to check the Nest feed, nothing came up."

"We checked that, too," Kate said. "The feed was killed."

"What?"

She knew she had to be careful here. The last thing she wanted was to inform him that his wife had slept with another man less than an hour or so before she was killed. If they truly believed Ashley Watts might be the killer, it would be pertinent information to share, but as it stood, Kate did not see the sense in putting him through such pain.

"We found it odd, too," DeMarco said, picking up on Kate's hesitation. "We're working to get it figured out with them."

"Do you recall how she was acting before you left for work yesterday?" Kate asked.

"She seemed normal. Perfectly fine. We ... we made love before I left for work. We were excited because it was going to be a short day at work for me. We had plans for a date last night and ..."

Kate could already sense that this little interview was going to be quick. She did not think David Lowell was going to make it very long.

"Mr. Lowell, how would you describe your marriage? Was it happy? Were there issues or strain?"

"We were very happy. Sure, I caught flak from people for being significantly older, but that was about it. Meredith seemed happy. And she made *me* happy."

"He's right," Paulette said from the edge of the room. "They were one of those couples that other couples hated to be around. They were annoyingly cute together."

"Yeah, I guess we were," Lowell agreed.

"What can you tell us about Meredith?" Kate asked. "What was she like? What interests and hobbies did she have? If we can find a link between her and the other two women who were murdered, it may help point us toward a suspect."

"Meredith was...well, she was a delight. God, she was such a *light.*"

As he chewed on his own words, Kate started to feel uncomfortable. Clearly he knew nothing about her other side—the side that had quick sex sessions with the delivery man every chance she could.

"She was a very big reader," Lowell went on. "She tore through about three books a month. Sometimes more. She was very interested in learning how to cook, though she would be the first to tell you she was never very good at it. She was a fan of classical music, something that always surprised me because she also likes nineties hip-hop. A weird combination, you know? But I think classical was her favorite. It's actually one of the things that drew me to her."

"How did you meet?" DeMarco asked.

"At a tacky bar down in Miami. I was on vacation and she was just sort of journeying around from place to place, taking a break from community college. It was a piano bar, right before it was closing up. I was headed out and heard someone sort of trying to play this classical piece that sounded familiar. I went to see who was playing it, and there she was. Her and a friend were sitting on the piano bench and Meredith was clumsily trying to play a song that I later figured out was Debussy's 'Clair de Lune.' And that was it..."

"Did she live in Florida or did she just go to school there?" Kate asked.

"She was born and raised in Mississippi. Did some community college and hated it. When I met her, she said she was *in between* classes."

"Was she not working as of late?"

"Not really. She did some virtual assistant work when she could find it. I had a friend set her up with this eBay business where she would buy stuff dirt cheap from resellers, catalogue them, and then sell them. But she was the one that wanted that. She insisted on it. I told her I didn't want my wife working if she didn't want to. I wanted her to have a life of luxury."

"And she was okay with that?"

"Most of the time. Sometimes I think she got restless and bored...but I think, overall, she was happy."

Restless and bored, Kate thought. *Two key ingredients for a spouse looking around for something else to do... namely an affair.*

Lowell lowered his head and took in a shuddering breath. A little sob came out and at first it seemed like that was the end of it. But then Kate saw the tremors and noticed that he would not look back up at them.

The interview was over. It had been all too brief, but Kate figured that was fine for now. For David Lowell to have been so oblivious to his wife's secret life, she doubted he'd be of much use for the remainder of the case anyway. But it was more than just a dent in the case; it was a dent in Kate trying to find a reason to buck against Duran's order to return back to DC.

Paulette gave Kate and DeMarco a little nod toward the hallway. Kate nodded as Bannerman was already headed out of the room to give Lowell his space.

"Thanks for your time, Mr. Lowell," Kate said as she and DeMarco walked out of the room. "Please give us a call if you happen to think of anything else that might help."

He was only able to give a weak nod as he gave in to his grief and let out a wail. He kicked helplessly at the floor, letting out his frustration in any way possible.

As Kate followed behind DeMarco toward the front door, she looked to the left, toward the den. There, the couch that Watts and Meredith Lowell had had sex on sat like some quiet witness. Kate frowned at it and then continued on her way to the door.

After two steps, she stopped. She cocked her head, as if listening for some idea that might be hovering in the air, and then stepped back toward the den. She gazed into the room, past the couch and the bookshelves, her eyes landing on the larger item in the room.

"DeMarco?"

"Yeah?" she asked, pausing at the front door as Bannerman held it open for her.

"The Hopkins residence … there was a piano, right?"

"There was, yes. The Hix family, too."

"That's what I thought…"

DeMarco walked back to join her, looking into the den. The piano sat near the back of the room, pushed into the corner with just enough room for someone to get on the bench behind it.

"What is it?" Paulette asked, coming up behind them.

"David said Meredith played a bit of piano," Kate said. "Did she play regularly?"

"I don't think so," Paulette said. "In fact, I doubt it. She was taking lessons from someone in the area from what David tells me."

"Any idea how long?"

Before she could answer, David came to the arched doorway of the living room. He did not step into the hallway, but leaned against the wall as if he might fall over. "About a month or so now," he said, apparently having heard the conversation.

"Do you have a name and number for the instructor?" Kate asked. She could sense DeMarco and Bannerman tensing up behind her, sensing that they may have just accidentally stumbled across a new lead.

"One second," he said. When he pushed himself away from the wall, he seemed to glide. He looked like he was being pushed gently down the hall rather than walking.

"You think there's something to this?" Paulette asked. "Did the other two women take piano lessons?"

Kate did not answer, as she did not want to give a hope that might not exist. But she could see the dens and living areas of those other two houses, could see the pianos situated in her mind as if she were standing on those rooms. Sure, it could be a coincidence, but it would have to be a damned strong one.

David came back to the den entrance with a business card in his hand. Kate took it and saw that the card itself was designed to look like piano keys, with the name and number of the instructor situated on different keys.

"Thomas Knudsen," Kate said. "You ever meet him?"

"Once. He was this really tall, very serious sort of man. Maybe about sixty years old if I had to guess. He was very pleasant, very happy." It then seemed to dawn on him why they were suddenly so interested in his late wife's piano lessons. He frowned and added: "No...no, I don't know if that makes sense. Tom is...I don't...well..."

Paulette took her brother by the arm and led him back toward the living room. "Agents, you can see he's wrecked. I promise you, he will call with any other information he thinks of."

"Thanks," Kate said, already heading for the door. The door had barely closed behind Bannerman before the three of them started to work together a plan.

"Knudsen," Bannerman said. "That's a pretty unique name. What is it...Polish, maybe?"

"Danish," DeMarco said.

"Whatever it is, it should make it very easy to locate him, even if he's in Chicago."

"I agree," Kate said. They had made it down the porch steps and back to the patrol car. Kate continued talking as they piled into the car, Bannerman pulling away from the curb with a little squeal of tires. "We've got two avenues here, and we need to knock them out quickly," she added.

Bannerman was already reaching for the little wireless mic attached to his dashboard. "I'll have someone at the station run his name, get an address to go along with the phone number on the card. See if he has an arrest record."

"We need to see if he's worked with Marjorie Hix or Karen Hopkins, too," DeMarco added.

"Sheriff, can you get your men on that while DeMarco and I pay Thomas Knudsen a visit?"

"Can do," Bannerman said with a twinge of excitement. And with that, he clicked the mic on and put in a request for Knudsen's home address and criminal record.

While Bannerman spoke to one of his officers, Kate looked at her phone and saw that it was 7:25. She was well aware that her time was running out and, with her time, perhaps the case. Hell, perhaps what remained of her little rebirthed career.

But she had to ignore that for now. Right now, there was just the case to focus on. She had to proceed as if they were on the verge of wrapping it and could not let the other drama she was currently dealing with get in the way.

That was, of course, easier said than done when she felt as if she was literally racing against the clock.

CHAPTER FIFTEEN

Kate and DeMarco made a quick stop at the station after having gotten their own car from the hotel. The Frankfield PD had already come through with quite a bit of information. They got their last bit, and perhaps the strongest, just as they were about to get back in the car and head to Knudsen's house.

"Hold up, Agents," Bannerman said, closing the door to the patrol car. He was speaking on the phone to someone, nodding enthusiastically. Kate couldn't help but feel slightly hopeful as she saw the look of promise on the sheriff's face. When he hung up and turned to them, that look of hope seemed magnified.

"Good news?" Kate asked.

"Good, and getting better. Thomas Knudsen does indeed have a criminal record. Petty misdemeanors, mostly. A bar fight a few years back, a domestic dispute with an ex-wife."

"How is he managing to find clients for piano lessons with a history like that?"

"I was literally just told that he only accepts adults as students. He was apparently a very highly respected concert pianist in Denmark up until about fifteen years ago ... not sure what happened to bring him to the states, though. Gerald Hopkins just told one of my guys over the phone that Knudsen charged Karen one hundred dollars per lesson."

"So he *did* give lessons to at least one of the other victims," DeMarco said.

"Yes. It's been confirmed. And we're trying to find out if there's that same link with Marjorie Hix right now."

"Thanks, Sheriff," Kate said.

Kate closed the door and sped out of the parking lot. She could not help but smile a bit at the sound of her tires squelching on the asphalt as she turned out onto the street. The little jolt of euphoria made her feel, if only for a moment, like she was DeMarco's age again, sniffing out the final stages of a case.

They sped out of Frankfield, heading in the direction of Chicago where, according to the address they had, they would turn off just shy of the city and drive into Chesterton. It was only a nineteen-minute drive but every minute that passed knocked that feeling of joy and youngness right out of Kate's sails.

"This has got to be the guy," DeMarco said as they turned off down a two-lane side street where modest homes lined the road. Off in the distance behind the homes, Lake Michigan sparkled almost magically in the morning sun.

"Seems to fit the bill," Kate said, though she was not ready to go all-in just yet. "He had access to the houses and is definitely some-one the women would invite in."

"His record, though…it doesn't really say *murderer,* does it?"

"I was thinking the same thing. But let's just see what Mr. Knudsen has to say about that."

As they neared the address, Kate could not help but press down on the accelerator. By the time they were on Knudsen's street, she was doing sixty miles per hour down a street with a twenty-five-mile-per-hour limit. As they headed down this final street, the glimmer of Lake Michigan shrank quite a bit and the houses started to look a little less spectacular. Still, the yards were much larger and more open than any they had seen so far on this case, perhaps given the room to display the promise of the lake properties several blocks to the right.

When Kate brought the car to a stop in front of Knudsen's house, it was 8:11. There was a car already parked in front of the house, perhaps belonging to Knudsen. Both women stepped out of the car and hurried up the sidewalk to what was a cute yet very modest-looking home. It was still likely in the mid six figures but not quite as high end as the houses they had visited in Frankfield.

As they came up onto the porch, they could hear piano music before they even approached the door. It had a crystalline sort of sound that instantly impressed Kate. The notes came fast, almost mathematically, and though it was quite beautiful it sounded more technical than musical to her ear.

She and DeMarco both took a moment to brace themselves before Kate knocked. Kate could tell from DeMarco's expression that she, too, felt that they could very well be on the precipice of breaking the case wide open—that they might have the murderer in custody within the next few minutes.

Kate knocked, but the piano music was loud enough to drown the knocking out. She knew it right away, so she knocked again. This time, it was harder and more persistent. The piano stopped and within seconds, they heard fast and thunderous footsteps nearing the door. When the door was answered it seemed to fly inward with a very tall and angry man standing on the other side. He was, as David Lowell had suggested, a bit on the older side, with several years on Kate.

"What could you *possibly* want this early in the morning?" the man said, his voice nearly in a shout. He was clearly angry, his eyes darting back and forth between them. Behind him, the piano music continued. He seemed to roll his eyes at it.

"Are you Thomas Knudsen?" Kate asked.

"I am. And currently, I am a very irate Thomas Knudsen. I am in the middle of a piano lesson and I had to stop to answer the door for such a stupid question."

"Here's a better one, then," Kate said, taking out her ID and flashing it nearly in front of his face. "Could you make time to answer some questions for the FBI?"

With the anger still on his face, Knudsen took a small step back. He looked at the badge and then to Kate, sneering. "What the hell for?"

"We'd much rather discuss this inside," Kate said.

"As I said, I'm in the middle of a lesson."

"Well, the lesson will have to be postponed. That, or we can just ask you a bunch of potentially damaging questions in front of your student."

"About what, exactly?" Knudsen challenged. "What the hell does the FBI want with *me*?"

Kate looked behind him, into the hallway beyond, as if suggesting she really wanted to come inside.

"I suppose if I reject your request to come inside, you'll eventually find your way in, through paperwork and phone calls to your superiors?"

"Yes. And the harder you make it for us, the harder we will make it for you."

"Well, damn. There's your answer then." He grunted as he stood to the side. "Hurry in, then, if it's so fucking important."

Kate nearly got mouthy right back with him but decided to stay on the high road. His language reminded her of his past charges and she wanted him to think she and DeMarco were simply servants, timid and just doing their jobs. She wondered how much about himself he might reveal if she allowed him to rely on his anger without correcting him.

He stormed back into the hallway, waving them on as he passed. He walked with those same pissed off, thundering steps as he led them into a large room that held only a gorgeous piano and a couch. A woman of about twenty-five or so sat behind the piano, taking everything in with extreme worry on her face. Knudsen basically threw himself on the couch in a far-too-dramatic fashion and looked at the lady behind the piano.

"Courtney, I'm sorry but we'll have to cancel the rest of the lesson. I'll add the forty-five minutes to your next lesson and maybe I can even get one of these rude ladies to pay for it."

"Do you—" the woman—Courtney, apparently—started to say.

"Not now, please," Knudsen said. "Tomorrow, same time."

"I have to work tomorrow morning."

"Figure it out then," he snapped. "It's *your* forty-five minutes."

Kate was about to interject, as he was nearly screaming at the poor woman. Courtney got up from the piano stool and made her exit, though. She barely looked at the agents as she made her way to the hall and toward the front door.

"I charge one hundred dollars per hour, per lesson," Knudsen said. "Are one of you prepared to make that up to me?"

"No, I'm sorry," Kate said sarcastically.

"It's not even nine in the morning," DeMarco said. "Isn't it a little early for piano lessons?"

"To the untalented, sure. But studies have shown that the practice of any art—particularly music—is best done in the morning. The brain is more adaptable to the memory of it all. My first lesson this morning was at six o'clock."

"Are all of your lessons out of your home?" Kate asked.

"No," he said, looking at her as if she had just burped in his face. "That would be stupid. I do about half of my lessons here and half at the homes of my clients. But what care is that of yours?"

"I'm glad you asked," DeMarco said.

"Mr. Knudsen," Kate said, "can you confirm that you have students by the names of Karen Hopkins, Marjorie Hix, and Meredith Lowell?"

"Not in actuality. I have not worked with Karen Hopkins in almost a year. She was not very good and gave up. I think it saved the world several headaches, if I'm being honest. But yes, Meredith and Marjorie are current clients. I have a lesson with Marjorie Hix later today. Not that it's any concern of yours. Is that why you're here? To get some sort of odd roll call?"

"Mr. Knudsen, those three women have all been killed within the past ten days," Kate said. "So it looks like your day just opened up a bit, huh?"

"What? This is a joke, yes?"

"No. All three of them are dead. And so far, the only concrete thing we have to link them all is that they took lessons with you."

Kate thought the shock on his face was genuine, but the anger and pompousness he had displayed since the moment they arrived was still very much on his face. "So then how can I help?" He paused here, as if letting the news truly catch up to him for the first time. "Karen was...well, she was a very nice woman. She had talent but was afraid to really dig it up..."

"We need to know when you last saw each woman, for starters," DeMarco said.

"I saw Marjorie just four days ago. She was here, right there on that bench, for a lesson."

"Did you ever go to her house for lessons?"

"No. It's always been here."

"And what about the others?"

"For Meredith and Karen, I did go to their homes. But as I said, it's been almost a year since I last saw Karen Hopkins."

"Do you have any proof of that?"

Again, he looked to Kate as if she had done something offensive. He let out a nervous laugh and said: "How am I supposed to prove that I have *not* seen someone?"

"Did the lessons end mutually, on a good foot?"

"Yes, it was her decision. She felt the money could be spent better elsewhere."

"What about Meredith Lowell?" DeMarco asked. "When did you last visit her home to give lessons?"

"Last week. Thursday, I believe."

"Did any of your clients give you passcodes or other access to their security systems?"

Genuinely confused now, Knudsen got to his feet and scowled at them. "Of course not. I'm a piano teacher, not a repairman. And quite honestly...I see where this line of questioning is headed. And it's *beyond* insulting."

Kate nodded, but slowly made her way over to the piano. She had taken a few lessons as a kid before she realized she did not have the patience or, quite frankly, the musical aptitude to be any good. She knew very little about the instrument, but the one in Knudsen's house was gorgeous. It was an older model Bosendorfer—a model Knudsen must have continuously poured money into in order to keep it sounding like it had when she and DeMarco had heard it from the porch. There was a single piece of sheet music on the holder above the keys. Kate couldn't even begin to read it, as it was far too complicated.

She paused, though, as she spotted three other items on the thin ledge that held the sheet music stand. There was a small, finely polished white seashell, the kind you could buy for a buck at any beach gift shop. There was also some old, faded coin—a buffalo nickel, she saw upon closer inspection. The third item cause her a moment of pause, one she could tell right away alarmed Knudsen.

And it should have.

It was the top portion of a stalk of cotton. While the cotton itself appeared to be real, the stalk on which it had been placed was very fake. It was the same sort that stocked the shelves of just about every hobby and craft store in the country.

And it was the exact same kind that Karen Hopkins had in her office. Kate could remember being drawn to the fake stalks as she and DeMarco had first investigated Karen Hopkins's office.

"This cotton seems rather random," Kate said. "You want to tell me where it came from?"

For the first time since they had arrived, Knudsen seemed to be shaken. He shook his head and took a step towards the wall.

"It was just a random thing I picked up at a craft store."

"It also happens to be the exact same fake cotton plant that sat in the office of Karen Hopkins. Did you know that?"

"Actually, yes, I did know that. And I see what you are insinuating..."

"Do you?"

He sighed here, doing a very good job of trying to play the victim. "So what if I did take it from Karen Hopkins's house? It's just a piece of fake cotton plant..."

"That's right. But as I said, the plant is in her office, where she died. The piano is in a completely different room. So why would you have any need to go into her office?"

"No reason, I just..."

He trailed off here, taking another step back. DeMarco fol-lowed him this time, keeping the same distance between them. Kate noted that now that he was truly worked up and starting to worry, she could hear a bit of a Danish accent coming out. She hadn't noticed one at all up until this point.

"Mr. Knudsen, we need you to come with us," DeMarco said. "Peacefully and cooperatively would be preferred."

"I think not. I've done nothing. I took a fragment of fake plant. How in the hell does that link me to a murder?"

He didn't realize it, but the rhetorical question was pretty dam-aging on his part. Kate took a few steps forward as she and DeMarco triangulated on him while he continued to back himself into a cor-ner. He started to look around for a means of escape but realized that his two errant steps backward had screwed him up quite badly.

In the end, he apparently decided that given he already had a record, there was no reason to fight. He simply bowed his head and offered his wrists. "Fine," he said with a shaky breath. "Fuck both of you, by the way."

"Very classy of you," Kate said, more than happy to take out her cuffs and apply them to his offered wrists.

Chapter Sixteen

Thomas Knudsen did not say a single word on the way from his home in Chesterton to the Frankfield police department. He was as still as a concrete slab as they transported him. DeMarco called Bannerman and gave him the update and in return, Bannerman told them a bit more information he and the police had dug up on Thomas Knudsen.

Knudsen left Denmark sixteen years ago after a brutally bad marriage that ended in a case of domestic violence. It truly was a shame, as he had been one of the country's foremost pianists, filling in on orchestras and playing infamous locations and venues for government-funded events. He had been in the studio with one of Denmark's most famous vocalists when his marriage had gone south, and after he'd come out of the mess of the divorce and the legal proceedings, he had come to America and lived in obscurity. He'd played in a few jazz bands in the New York area before ultimately choosing a quiet life by the Great Lakes, where he had floated around the Chicago area, ultimately landing in Chesterton seven years ago. He'd been teaching piano lessons all that time, also working on some freelance work for small film studios.

As Kate led Knudsen into the precinct, it was hard to imagine such a successful life trailing behind this curmudgeonly old man. But she supposed she could identify; she had her own life that had also quickly gotten behind her, a past that even now would not let go of her in the form of a career.

Bannerman led the way, making silent cues to the officers they passed not to stand and stare. They obeyed for the most part, and

Kate could see that Knudsen was starting to look embarrassed. Still, he did not utter a single word as they came to the interrogation room and remained equally silent as Bannerman sat him down in the single chair behind the small table.

"Mr. Knudsen," Kate began, "we need to know everything about your relationship with those three women. Every little detail."

"I'm sure you do," he said. "But as you have infringed upon my rights, I'm afraid I won't say a single word to any of you until I have my lawyer present."

"You really want to play it that way?" Bannerman asked. "Makes you look guilty as far as I'm concerned."

"I'm no idiot, Sheriff. I know how your corrupted system works in this backwards country. If three women are dead, as you all say they are, and I am the only link between them, the media will make their assumptions and I will be made out to be a villain. Which would be a shame for you, your department, and even the FBI. Because as you will find out soon enough, depending on your level of skill, I'm innocent."

"That's for us to determine," DeMarco said.

"And I'll be happy to help you reach that conclusion ... once my lawyer is here."

Bannerman looked furious, but clapped his hands firmly to his hips and started pacing back and forth across the room. Kate knew that Knudsen was within his rights to wait on his lawyer and she would typically be fine with that. But she knew Duran would be waiting for her in DC, that he would start to get suspicious if she didn't show up by noon or so.

"Sheriff, can I see you outside?" she said.

He nodded and opened the door with a bit too much force and anger for Kate's taste. Kate and DeMarco followed him out into the hallway, where he seemed to instantly calm down a bit.

"First things first," Kate said. "Get someone to hand Knudsen a phone and let him call his lawyer. Let him feel as if he's running the show. In the meantime, that piece of cotton we found in his house is bigger trouble for him than he realizes. We have enough speculative evidence to assume that it came from the Hopkins residence."

"Not to mention he even admitted to it," DeMarco said.

"Right. So that, plus his admitted link to all three victims, gives us more than enough evidence to support a full investigation of his home. Sheriff, if you can get some men on that right now, I'd like to continue trying to press him. If we can get some more evidence together before his lawyer makes it here, his hole gets even deeper."

"You're welcome to try," Bannerman said, "but it seems to me that he's made up his mind to be quiet until his lawyer gets here."

"Just let me handle that. In the meantime, give him what he wants. Let him call his lawyer."

Bannerman nodded and hurried off to set someone to the task. DeMarco gave Kate a skeptical look, one that was punctuated with the thinnest angle of a grin. "You got a plan brewing?"

"Not really. I just don't have the time to be yanked around by a lawyer right now."

DeMarco looked like she was about to say something but then bit it back. She then sighed and took a step closer to Kate. "Duran called me last night and told me he asked you to step down off of the case. He asked me to make sure to keep him posted if you showed any signs of not following the rules."

"I see. So did you call him yet to rat me out?"

"No. And I'm not going to. So get in there and do whatever it is you have in mind. How long do you think we have until Duran figures out that you went against orders?"

"Maybe three hours."

"You think Knudsen is our guy?"

Kate thought about it for a moment and then shrugged. "I honestly don't know. If it weren't for that damned stalk of cotton, I wouldn't have even given him a second thought—aside from his being an ass and all."

DeMarco nodded. "He does pretty much fit all of the slots we're trying to fill."

Kate nodded and turned back toward the interrogation room door. "Let's see if we can fill a few more."

❧ ❧ ❧

Kate had sat silently while Knudsen had called his lawyer. She'd stared at him during the entirety of the conversation, her gaze relaxed and nonchalant. Knudsen eyed her viciously as he spoke, breaking eye contact with her only once he had killed the call and slid the phone back to the officer who had given it to him.

When the officer left the room, DeMarco came in and took his place. Knudsen looked to her and back to Kate. "What, exactly, are you looking at?"

"A man who seems to have all the time in the world," Kate said. "I, on the other hand, have no time to spare. Three women are dead and, if I'm being honest, I have a supervisor that is riding my ass for not having many answers. When did your lawyer say he'd be here?"

"About an hour and a half. Am I expected to sit here until then?"

"Yeah. Shame he's going to take so long. As I said, I don't have the time to waste either. It might save us both the time and headache if you just tell me everything you can."

"I have already told all of you that I will not say another word until my lawyer is here."

"Well, here's the deal. That cotton stalk you took from the Hopkins residence, along with your own verification that you worked with all three of the victims, gives us more than enough cause to search your home, no warrant needed. So right now, as we wait for your slow lawyer, Sheriff Bannerman and a few of his men are headed to your house right now. So between just the three of us right now, can you tell me if they'll find anything else?"

"That isn't legal." Although it was a curt statement, he did not sound so sure.

"Oh, it is. Just ask your lawyer...when he gets here."

Knudsen started to look panicked for the first time. He looked trapped, coming to the realization that no matter how much of an asshole he tried to be, he was no longer in control of this situation—if he ever was.

"Whatever you have, share it now and it might make it easier on you."

Knudsen looked so angry that Kate thought he could probably chew nails in that moment. "You're enjoying this, aren't you?"

"Me? Visiting this part of the country to look into why three women were murdered? No … I don't enjoy it, to be honest."

"Mr. Knudsen," DeMarco said, "if you did not kill those women, then anything else you share with us—anything criminal—is not going to hurt. If anything, some judges may see it as assistance to a case. Do you understand that?"

"I did *not* kill them."

"Help us believe you, then," Kate said. "Because if there is anything worth finding, Bannerman and his men *will* find it."

Knudsen looked at both agents and then at the ceiling, casting his eyes anywhere but the accusing eyes in front of him. "The cotton stalk … it was stupid," he said. His voice was no longer laced with so much anger, but now harbored what sounded like genuine regret and embarrassment. It was one of the quickest switches in emotion Kate had ever seen in an interrogation room, making her wonder if Knudsen's angry façade was mostly fake—all a show to support the stereotypical introverted lifestyle of a musician.

"So why'd you take it?" DeMarco asked.

"I'm sure you know I have a record. Petty theft. Public disturbances and things like that. Nothing serious. But the theft … I've been doing it since I was a kid, you know? I never had issues with drinking, drugs, or sex. It was always stealing. But I never stole anything major … just dumb shit here and there."

"Like what?" Kate asked.

"Like Karen's cotton stalk. Like a pack of guitar strings when I was touring with a small band in Denmark. A bottle of perfume from an old lover. The most expensive thing I ever stole was an iPod off of someone on a plane back in 2010 or so. It had dropped in the floor and I snatched it up. Serves me right that it was filled with far too much of the garbage that serves as today's popular music, I suppose."

"Did you take things from the homes of the other victims, Marjorie Hix and Meredith Lowell?"

Knudsen frowned as he nodded. "I've taken something from every home I've taught a lesson in. I took a few marbles from the Hix home—those decorative kind of flat marbles people use to fill vases, you know?"

"And the Lowells?" DeMarco asked.

"She came to me for the lessons, remember? I never once went into her home. Other homes I've instructed in, though—I'd take things like magazines, little knickknack type things on their mantels, things like that. Never anything big or worth getting into a fuss about."

"Are these things hidden in your home, or sort of out in the open like the cotton stalk?" Kate asked.

"No, they're not locked away or anything. Marjorie's marbles are located on the kitchen counter, next to another client's small creamer container that I took from her kitchen."

Kate relaxed a bit, feeling that his sudden surge of honesty toward these things would have softened him up, making it easier for him to discuss other things.

"Thanks for that," Kate said, nodding to DeMarco. DeMarco took the hint and stepped outside, already taking out her phone to call Bannerman and fill him in. When DeMarco was out with the door closed behind her, Kate pressed a bit harder. "All of that information, at first glance, would make most assume that you are indeed the killer. Would you be able to give me alibis for the times in which the women were killed?"

"Who was the most recent?" Knudsen had resigned himself to defeat. He did not seem interested in his lawyer anymore. He honestly didn't seem too concerned about much of anything. He looked lost, beaten, and like he just wanted to go back home.

"Meredith Lowell. She was killed yesterday morning in her home. We don't have an approximate time, but it appears to have been done between nine and eleven thirty in the morning."

"I had three lessons yesterday morning, two at my home and the third out in the city. The first was at six thirty, the second was at eight, and the one out in Chicago was at ten. Following that last lesson, I went to the Dusty Groove, this record store that has a surprisingly impressive collection of classical on vinyl."

"Any idea when you got home?"

"Maybe noon? A little after, perhaps."

"Would you be willing to give us the names of the clients you worked with yesterday?"

Here, Knudsen looked a little more nervous. She thought she saw a twitch of that anger creeping back in. "No, for that I really would prefer for my lawyer to be here."

Kate knew not to push again. She'd gotten more than she'd expected from him—perhaps enough to eliminate him altogether, though that might not be the case until they got the names of the clients.

"Did you buy anything at the record store?"

"Yes. Two albums."

"How did you pay?"

"Cash. Straight out of one of the one-hundred-dollar bills I'd earned that morning."

"I don't suppose you kept the receipt?"

"Maybe. If I did, it's still in the pocket of the pants I wore yesterday."

Kate didn't bother pointing out that the receipt could very well be enough to free him. There might be a time discrepancy—perhaps about half an hour or so for him to have showed up at the Lowells' before venturing into the city—but she already knew that was a desperate grasp.

"Did you—"

"No more until my lawyer gets here."

"Okay."

She got up and started for the door and was surprised when Knudsen spoke up before she could so much as reach for the handle.

"I could have handled it better," he said. "You two, arresting me. I sort of backed up … panicked. I knew the theft was dumb and … I don't know. I've never been able to beat it. It's fucking embarrassing. It's …"

He stopped here and waved her away dismissively. Kate finally made it out the door, stepping out into the hallway where DeMarco was giving Bannerman the specifics. Kate sighed and gave her a quick shake of the head. DeMarco wrapped up the call quickly, the frown on her face an indication that she understood what Kate's shake of the head meant.

"What did you get?"

"Enough to know he's not the killer. A bit of a bipolar asshole, sure. But not the killer. I imagine Bannerman and his men will have enough to back that up by the end of the day. Do you mind calling him back and asking him to check the dirty clothes? Look for a pair of jeans. Check the front pockets for a receipt from a record store yesterday."

With that instruction, DeMarco's face fell slightly as she understood that they would soon be back to ground zero, with no clues or worthwhile leads. Kate realized it, too. She now had a little less than three hours before Duran would be on to her and, she feared, this little experiment with a resurrected career would be over.

"You know," DeMarco said as the phone rang in her ear, "as far as I'm concerned, he's our guy. Until some damning piece of evidence comes forward …"

She stopped here as Bannerman answered the call on the other end. Kate understood her optimism and wished she felt the same. But as it stood, she felt certain Knudsen was not their man. Still, she could not help but think of those three pianos, parked in each house like hidden giants, out in the open yet overlooked, quiet but with a story to tell.

Slowly, she started down the hallway toward the exit. She waved DeMarco along with her and her partner reluctantly followed. She was growing irritated now, and not doing much to hide the fact.

Kate didn't blame her. Duran basically had DeMarco babysitting her and she was trying to be a friend by doing a lousy job. So far, Kate had been doing nothing but making her regret that.

When they had reached the parking lot and headed for the car, DeMarco's second call with Bannerman was over. "Where are we going?" DeMarco asked.

"To check on a hunch."

"You sure it's not just grasping at invisible straws so you don't get reamed out in three hours?"

The comment stung but Kate figured she deserved it. "No," she said, shrugging the sting away. "Can I ask you to just trust me on something?"

"On what? Kate, where the hell are we going?"

"To look at some pianos."

CHAPTER SEVENTEEN

When Kate knocked on the door of the Hopkins home fifteen minutes later, she did not expect an answer, and she did not get one. There were no vehicles in the driveway and the place had the same feel she had gotten from the Lowell house yesterday—the feeling of sorrow and abandonment.

She had held on to the key Bannerman had given them when they had first met. It was hard to think that it had only been a few days ago. When she unlocked the door and stepped inside, she gave a cautionary "Hello" to anyone who might be inside. The only thing that came back to her was a hollow noise that was not quite her echo.

"Even if Knudsen turns out not to be the killer," Kate said, "the fact remains that there was a piano in each home. It may seem like a small detail at first but, really, what is the percentage of homes you visit that have a piano?"

"I don't know," DeMarco said. "I've never really thought of it. Far less than half, for sure."

They stepped into the den and strode over to the piano. As Kate stood beside it, she peered into the room directly attached to the den—the room that had once been an office for Karen Hopkins. From where she stood, she could see the vase containing the cotton stalks in the corner, a few of the stalks broken off.

"You know much about pianos?" Kate asked DeMarco.

"Virtually nothing. Not even Chopsticks."

"I tinkered with it for a while when I was a kid," Kate said. She started to circle the piano, a little disappointed in herself that she

125

had nearly overlooked the damned thing the first time they had visited. She did remember being a bit awestruck by the piano in the Hix home—a baby grand Steinway.

"Is this a nice one?" DeMarco asked.

Kate sat down at the bench behind the keys. The cover was raised, the keys exposed and inviting. "I'm not too sure. It looks to be of a good quality. I'd hate to guess on the price, though."

"What are we looking for?" DeMarco asked. "Or was I right? Are you just… grasping?"

"There might be *some* grasping," Kate admitted.

She sighed and rested her fingers on the keys. The feel of it brought a smile to her face. She had not even attempted to play in over ten years. Lazily, almost as if mocking her younger self, she slowly started to plink away at the first few notes of Beethoven's "Fur Elise." Her smile widened as the notes came out. She played slowly, messing up a few notes almost right away. It was not at all like riding a bicycle; apparently, you did not retain much, especially over the span of thirty-five years or so.

She played no more than ten seconds of the song before she gave up. Just as she did, though, she hit a key that did not make a sound. It was almost as if her finger had skipped over it. She hit the key again and got the same thing.

A dead note. Maybe she *was* grasping. Maybe she was…

She looked back down at the keys. She reached back down and hit the key in question for a third time, middle C. It was indeed dead—not making the slightest sound other than some sad little thump inside the body.

"What is it?" DeMarco asked.

"This C… it's dead. It's not making a noise at all."

"Is that uncommon?"

"It is for pianos that are in regular use. Someone like Karen Hopkins, who we know at least had a vague interest in playing, doesn't strike me as someone that would allow her piano to be out of tune… much less suffering from a dead key. It's almost like the wire has snapped." She ran her fingers down a few scales on the keys, frowning. "And this C seems to be the only key with that problem."

"Sorry... but I don't see how this is a big deal."

Kate hit the key again, her thoughts churning. "It might not be. But it could also be pretty damned big if..."

"If what?"

"Feel like a taking a trip over to the Hix residence?"

"Will you be able to finally make some sense while we're there?"

"Hopefully."

"Then by all means, let's go."

Kate realized she was likely coming off as distant and maybe even rude, but she didn't care in that moment. A theory was piling up in her head and she feared if she spoke it out loud or did any sort of overthinking, it would unravel. But DeMarco, God bless her, was going along and simply trusting her—even if she was doing so in absolute silence as they got back into the car.

Kate did not have a key for the Hix house so she had to call Bannerman to have an officer meet them. He did one better and met them himself just seven minutes after they arrived. He pulled in behind their car, giving the *For Sale* sign in the yard a curious glance. Kate gave it the same sort of stare. It had not been there when they had visited two days ago. Apparently, the realty company was trying to move fast.

"You think you got something here?" Bannerman asked.

"I don't know yet. Just wanting to test out a theory."

"Well, I hope you have something because Knudsen's place was a bust. We found everything you told us he mentioned. But there was no sign of a receipt from a record store."

"And he won't give the names of his clients from yesterday morning until his lawyer gets there," Kate said.

"Still... pretty impressive you got what you did out of him."

With that, Bannerman unlocked the front door to the Hix residence and the three of them walked inside. Kate wasted no time, walking directly into the large room that wanted badly to be a den of some sort but looked more like a pretentious sitting room or study, tucked to the left of everything else in the open floor plan house.

She was vaguely aware of Bannerman and DeMarco whispering to one another—likely Bannerman asking her partner what in the hell her older partner was doing. The piano had struck her as beautiful the first time and it did not disappoint as she sat down behind it. The baby grand Steinway seemed to make her feel taller, like she could play anything she wanted.

She resisted the urge to try "Fur Elise" again. This time, she simply ran her fingers down the length of the keys, white and black alike. She tapped each note, listening for anything that might be off.

A little more than halfway down, she was halted by another dead note. This time, because she was expecting it, the lack of music from the key felt irritating somehow—like scratching her nails down a chalkboard. Kate looked back down at the keys and, just like that, she knew her hunch was right.

This missing note was a B—and it was the key directly beside the dead C she had found at the Hopkins residence.

She felt DeMarco slowly approaching her from behind. "I know nothing about piano, but that was dead, right?"

"Right. It was a B... the key directly beside the C that was off with Karen Hopkins's piano."

Now Bannerman was beside her as well, looking down at the piano as if he thought it might come alive and bite him. "So what, exactly, does that mean?"

"It means these women would have needed piano tuners or repairmen to come fix it. Hopkins I could let slide because she hadn't been an active player in a year or more—at least that's what I ascertained from Knudsen. But she might have been playing just for fun at home, I suppose. But we know that Marjorie Hix was actively taking lessons, and inside of her home, with Knudsen. Now, if that was the case, how could she possibly practice on a piano with a dead key?"

"So you think we're looking for someone who tunes pianos?"

"Yeah, but not a fish," DeMarco said. She was cringing as soon as it was out of her mouth. She gave a quick and embarrassed "I'm sorry" before looking at the floor.

"Yes, a tuner or some sort of maintenance person. And while we're looking for local piano tuners, I think I'd like to speak with the coroner."

"Why's that?" Bannerman asked.

"I'm wondering if it would be possible to strangle someone with a piece of piano wire."

With that comment in the air, they all looked at the piano with the same sort of caution Bannerman had given it moments ago.

CHAPTER EIGHTEEN

The medical examiner in charge of the Hopkins and Hix cases had just started digging into the Lowell case. Meredith Lowell's body was still on his table but he seemed hesitant to allow Kate and DeMarco into the room.

"There are things I still don't quite understand about the death," he said. He was a rotund and rather short man named Fenn. Kate decided right away that she liked him simply because of his respect for the dead. She had encountered far too many MEs and coroners who were more than happy to show off the latest body.

"Like what exactly?" DeMarco asked.

They were standing outside of the examination room, Fenn standing directly in front of the door like some stout sentry.

"Well, for one, what the hell was used to strangle her. It has definition to it that I've just never seen before."

"Then maybe we can help," Kate said. "I have a theory I'm working on that could not only answer your question but, if I'm right, can probably make it much easier for us to find a killer."

Fenn looked back to the door and then sagged his shoulders. "Okay, it's fine. Come on in. I've got the files on Marjorie Hix and Karen Hopkins up on my tablet, too. The wounds were so similar, I had to at least assume they were all connected."

"We're certain they are," Kate confirmed.

The three of them stepped into the examination room where Meredith Lowell's body lay face-up on Fenn's table. There had been no autopsy yet, though most of the lights over the table had been directed to the wounds on her neck.

Kate stepped up to the table with a great deal of respect; she had long ago come to the conclusion that you never truly got used to looking over a dead body with a critical eye. Even those with the most professional of approaches must also remember that this person had once been alive—a living, breathing mother or brother or sister or father. She noticed that once Fenn saw her tentative attitude toward Meredith's body, he seemed to relax.

"What was your first thought?" Kate asked him.

"Honestly? A few years back I had a case where some guy strangled his neighbor to death with that plastic-looking weed-eater line. It looked quite similar to what we see here on Ms. Lowell's neck."

"Are the abrasions on the necks of Hix and Hopkins entirely similar or are there differences?"

Fenn smirked a bit and grabbed his tablet from the small counter on the backside of the room. "You know, there are some differences…though they are quite minute—so small that I didn't even notice until I started looking through a magnifying lens. But before I get into those specifics, why don't you tell me your theory?"

Looking at the marks and abrasions on Meredith Lowell's neck, Kate started to feel quite confident in her theory, right down to the dead notes on the pianos she had sat down behind this morning.

"I wonder if it might be possible to strangle someone with piano wire. There are urban legends of assassins using it as a weapon of choice for garrote-style killings, but I very seriously doubt we're dealing with an assassin here."

"It would be very easy," Fenn said, his eyes widening a bit at the possibility. "And it would explain the cuts on the neck of Karen Hopkins. With piano wire, if you squeeze tight enough, and, I imagine if there was some fight-back from the victim, piano wire would cut into flesh quite easily."

He showed Kate and DeMarco two pictures side by side on his tablet. One of them was labeled Hopkins, K; the other was Hix, M. Side by side, they did look identical.

"Now, after magnifying these wounds, it becomes apparent that the weapon that was used was not the same in each case. When I got in there and measured, it was apparent that the weapon used for strangulation was different in each case, from Hopkins to Lowell. The wounds were getting a bit thicker with each death, but not by much, we're talking millimeters here. But under magnification, it's quite clear."

"Different notes," Kate said.

"I beg your pardon?"

DeMarco picked up on it, explaining as best she could with a dawning excitement in her eyes. "He used a different string with each woman." She looked at Kate and said: "I have no idea how the inner workings of a piano are put together. Are the strings different sizes?"

"I'm not sure," Kate said, looking back to the fresh wounds on Meredith Lowell's neck. "But...I know someone who would."

Kate and DeMarco stayed busy on the telephone as they drove back to the station to speak with Thomas Knudsen. DeMarco was behind the wheel, mainly because Kate was convinced DeMarco was a better driver under pressure than she was. That left Kate available to make a series of calls that she hoped would fill in some blanks before they spoke with Knudsen again.

The first call she made was to Joseph Hix. When he answered the phone, it sounded like he had just woken up. It was a reminder to Kate that though she and DeMarco were being driven and motivated by these new breaks, she was still speaking with men who were grieving the loss of their wives.

"Mr. Hix, it's Agent Kate Wise," she said. "I hate to bother you, but I have one very strange-sounding question for you...but a question that might help us figure out who killed your wife."

"Of course. What is it?"

"Do you recall your wife ever mentioning the piano being out of tune?"

"Yes, actually. Pretty recently, in fact."

"Do you know if she hired someone to fix it?"

"I don't...I don't think so. She just complained about it being out of tune. If she hired a tuner, she did it without telling me. Which really wouldn't be all that unusual."

"I see," Kate said. "Well, thank you very much."

She ended that call and instantly flipped through the electronic files on her phone until she came to the number for David Lowell. It rang twice before it was answered by a familiar voice—Paulette Ivans, David's sister.

"This is David's phone," Paulette said. "May I ask who's calling?"

"Paulette, this is Agent Wise. I need to ask David a question."

"I don't know that he's up for it. He hasn't slept well and I'm having to beg him to eat."

"I understand that, but this is just *one* question and it could be pivotal to finding out who killed his wife."

Paulette took a moment to consider, sighed, and then gave in. "One second."

There was some shuffling, a murmured conversation, and then David Lowell was on the line. His voice came out in an exhausted whisper when he said, "Agent Wise?"

"Mr. Lowell, I'm so sorry to disturb you. But this is pressing and could be very important to the case. Can you remember any time in the recent past where Meredith might have mentioned needing someone to come tune the piano in your home?"

"She did. I don't know how long ago, though. Maybe a week. Maybe just a few days before..."

"Mr. Lowell...did she ever hire anyone to actually come and do it?"

"I don't know. Not that I can remember. I actually... I'm pretty sure she didn't. I just don't know. I can maybe check her calendar or the bank account info to see if she paid anyone or..."

He trailed off here, lost in the details of what had once seemed like nothing more than daily tasks.

"If you happen to figure it out, that would be great. In the meantime, can I speak with your sister again?"

"Sure," he said, his voice barely audible. He sounded relieved to have escaped the conversation.

"Hello?" Paulette asked moments later.

"I do apologize for that. I asked him for information that I don't think he's currently capable of finding for me. Given that, I wonder if you might do me a favor. Could you look around the house—maybe on the kitchen bar or the fridge—and see if you can find a business card or scrawled note about a piano tuner?"

"Um ... okay?"

"I know it sounds strange, but it would be an immense help."

"Okay," Paulette said, though she sounded distant. "I'll take a look."

"And one more thing ... while I have you on the phone."

"What is it?"

"This might sound equally odd, but could you go to the piano in the den?"

"What for?"

"Please ... trust me. I need you to help me with a little experiment. Do you know how to play?"

"Barely. A few lessons as a kid and nothing more."

"Do you know the basic location of the notes?"

"More or less. What is this all about?"

"I want you to start at the middle C and go a few keys over to the right, one by one. If you don't find anything off there, do the same to the left."

"Are you serious right now?"

"I am. And if you need an explanation, I can give it to you later. Right now, I just don't have the time."

"Fine."

Kate did her best to ignore the skepticism in Paulette's voice and listened as she walked her fingers down the notes of the treble scale. The ones to the right sounded fine, every single one of the six notes she played. She then stopped and then did the same on the opposite side of middle C just as Kate had asked. This time, after just two notes, including the middle C itself, there was a silent space. A dead note.

"That's the A, right?" Kate asked.

"Yes. How the hell did you know?"

Kate gave a quick thank you and ended the call. "We've got a dead note at the Lowell residence, too. The A this time."

"This is getting creepy," DeMarco said.

Kate nodded as she tried Gerald Hopkins's number. His phone rang three times and then went to voicemail. Kate left a message, instructing him to call her with an urgent matter, and then ended that call, too.

"All dead ends on the piano tuner front?"

"Not totally dead. I spoke with Hix and Lowell. They both recalled their wives commenting that the pianos needed tuning, but they don't remember anything ever actually being done about it."

"So their wives mentioned the need for them to be tuned but..."

"But it was apparently never done. And that could be because the tuner came with no intention of tuning the pianos at all."

"So now we just need to find the tuner," DeMarco commented.

"And hopefully that's another area our friend Thomas Knudsen can be of assistance."

The comment weighed heavy in the car as DeMarco continued to speed toward the station, her speed making Kate very aware that her time was quickly running out.

CHAPTER NINETEEN

When they got back to the station, Knudsen's lawyer had still not arrived. Knudsen looked irritated and a bit bored when Kate and DeMarco entered the room. After a few seconds, though, he looked hopeful—like he hoped their return might mean that he could go free. As far as Kate was concerned, it was yet another sign of his innocence.

"Mr. Knudsen," Kate said, "I can understand that you are not happy with your situation. And, between you, myself, and Agent DeMarco, we have discovered a few things this morning that make me view you less and less as a suspect."

"Well, it's about damned time," he spat.

Kate completely ignored this and went on. "Mr. Knudsen, we find ourselves in a position where you could help us. We need your expertise to clear up a few things that might help us nail down a killer."

"Help you? After the hell you've put me through this morning? Why in the hell would I do that?"

"I think she just explained that," DeMarco said. "To help us find a killer."

"Someone has killed three women for no good reason," Kate said. "Three women that you knew. I would appreciate your help in answering just a few questions about what you do for a living. Is that really too much to ask?"

Kate had delivered similar sentiments numerous times in her career and it almost always worked. The art of making someone feel that you will be lost without them tended to inflate the ego. And honestly, Kate didn't even think it was necessary with Knudsen. The more certain he became that he was going to be let go, the more he seemed to soften up, making it clear that the tough guy asshole schtick really was mostly a front.

"What do you need to know?" he asked.

"Do you know of any piano tuners in the Frankfield area? Maybe even as far out as Chicago?"

"Not personally. I've always tuned my own pianos; I have since I was a teenager."

"That's almost as good," DeMarco said. "What can you tell us about the strings inside? They're all different sizes, right?"

"Yes. Some of the differences in sizes are so minuscule, though, that you wouldn't even notice it unless you were a real pro or knew what to look for."

"So let's say you look at a C string, a B string, and an A string all from the same scale. The variation in the size of the wires might not be all that noticeable, right?"

"Well, you might see a difference between the C and the A pretty easily *if* you even knew to look. Why are you asking me about this?"

Kate looked at DeMarco, having one of those little unspoken conversations. DeMarco shrugged, as if to say: *What could it hurt?*

"Mr. Knudsen," Kate said, "we are fairly certain the killer is strangling his victims with piano wire. We have been told by two of the three victims' husbands that their wives had indeed mentioned their pianos being out of tune... one of whom even said his wife had mentioned reaching out to a tuner. So... are you *certain* you don't know of any tuners?"

"Again, not personally," Knudsen said. "But I know of one off-handedly. A student of mine mentioned him a few months back. I offered to do it for him, but he balked at what I was charging for it."

"Did he give you a name for this man?" Kate asked.

"No. Sorry."

From the sound of his voice, Kate thought he actually meant it; he was bummed that he could not help further.

"Mr. Knudsen...I know you did not want to give the names of students earlier, but this one could be huge. Please...can we have the name of the student that mentioned this tuner?"

Knudsen thought about it for a moment and then sighed, slouching in his chair. "His name was Barry Turner. An older guy that lives here in Frankfield. Good guy. Shows promise but he's a bit dramatic."

"Thank you, Mr. Knudsen. Now...how about an address?"

"Of course. First, though...how about you take these damned handcuffs off?"

Kate didn't even hesitate before opening the door to the interrogation room, poking her head out into the hall, and calling for anyone that could unlock Knudsen's cuffs.

CHAPTER TWENTY

He did not know why, but stepping into his workshop reminded him of stepping into the small-town library where he had spent most of his youth. The smell was sort of the same, the silence of the place was exactly the same, and he knew he was going to get lost in the aisles that sat in front of him. Of course, the aisles in his workshop were vastly different from the aisles of that long-ago library; instead of books, there were the hollowed out bodies of pianos. Most were from flea markets and yard sales. One was even from a yard sale in some rich Chicago suburb, a great find that he'd only dropped one hundred bucks on.

He walked through his workshop now, extending his hands and touching each of the pianos he had collected. There were nine in all, lined up on opposite sides of his cellar workshop. They all smelled of dust and neglect, but he liked to think of all of the beautiful music they had created over the years—of all of the talented fingers that had touched the keys (though five of these bodies didn't even have the majority of their keys intact).

He figured most craftsmen would have given up on these shells. But he had always seen beauty in ruin. He'd always been drawn to the piano, ever since he had learned to walk. Something so big and majestic, capable of making whispering crystalline noises and deep bass-like drones. And even when out of tune and mostly wrecked, there was still something beautiful about them. So much potential. So much promise.

He went to the next to last piano on the right side of the workshop space and sat on the makeshift bench he had created. The top of the piano was opened, the inside covered by a clear plastic tarp. He removed the tarp and exposed the strings inside. Again, he grew enamored. The inner workings of a piano were, to him, just as complicated as the human brain or heart. Yet, on the other hand, the strings inside were so easy to manipulate and shape. He looked at them now, the strings recently tuned by his own hands—his skills taking something that had been forgotten and gone to dust and transforming it into a thing of beauty.

He reached inside his coat pocket and took out a small baggie and a small set of tweezers. He opened the baggie and used the tweezers to carefully remove what was inside: a single strand of blonde hair, taken from the head of a woman named Meredith Lowell. He took great care and caution to place the hair onto the A string along the middle scale. As he did so, he tried not to get too distracted from the other strands of hair on the two keys next to it—hairs from Marjorie Hix and Karen Hopkins respectively.

He worked with his fingers and with the tweezers to tightly spool the hair around the piano string. It was a meticulous process, one that he assumed was much like making one of those ridiculous ship-in-a-bottle things. When it was wound perfectly and tightly some six minutes later, he took a moment to admire the loops and coils of the hair, like some thin sliver of magic on the string. He experimentally struck the key to make sure the hair would not come untangled or jostled. He smiled when it stayed unmoved.

The immense satisfaction he took from this was like waking up from some very long and much needed nap. He stared at the string a bit longer before covering the top back with the tarp but leaving the lid up.

After all, he'd be back under it very soon.

With that thought in mind, he walked back down his aisle of piano bodies and up the stairs. He walked through his very empty house and picked up his landline phone. He took the receiver from the cradle and dialed. As the phone rang in his ear, a little coil of excitement started to churn inside of him.

A woman picked up on the other end after four rings. "Hello?"

"Hi, is this Anna Forester?" he asked. Already, his hands were clenching; his right hand grasped the receiver while his free hand made a fist that opened and closed, opened and closed.

"It is. Who is this?"

He gave his name, giving it in the lighthearted, singsong sort of way he always did. "I got your message about your console piano. Sorry it's taken me so long to get back to you, but it's been a crazy week."

"It's no worry," Anna said. "Are you still available?"

"I am. I actually have a chunk of time available this afternoon and I'm headed out your way, in fact. I know it's short notice, but how about two? Could we work that out?"

"I believe so. I have to step out in a moment, but I should be back home by then. Does that work for you?"

His hands were still clenching and unclenching, anxious to get to work. With a smile on his face, he said: "That's perfect."

CHAPTER TWENTY ONE

It was 11:15 when Kate and DeMarco pulled up in front of Barry Turner's home. He lived in a respectable neighborhood, though a few steps down from what they had been seeing so far during this case. It was an old two-story brick home, the kind that looked aged and worn but in a charming sort of way. There was ivy climbing up one of the side of the house, as well as the worn white fence that separated Turner's yard from his neighbor's. The yard was covered in trees, the sidewalk covered in shadows from the branches.

As they approached the front door, Kate could hear piano music. It was not the same as when they visited Knudsen's residence; it was obvious from the sound and volume that this was a piano piece being played through a speaker, at a relatively high volume.

Kate knocked on the door, rapping loudly to be heard over the music. She was met with a "be right there" right away, coming from a cheerful voice with a musical quality. The door was answered several seconds later by an older gentleman with messy white hair. The hair was the only thing messy about him, though; his kind-looking face was closely shaved and he was dressed in a button-up shirt and a pair of casual khakis.

"Can I help you?" he asked, looking back and forth between Kate and DeMarco.

"Are you Barry Turner?" DeMarco asked.

"Guilty," he said with a smile.

"We got your name from your piano teacher, Thomas Knudsen," Kate said. "We're looking for information on someone and he thinks you might be able to help. Do you have a moment to speak with us?"

"Of course, come on in," he said. His tone was somewhere between concern and delight, betraying that musical tone to his voice.

The front door led almost directly into a little parlor area. It was here that the music was blaring through a Bose speaker. It was a classical piece that Kate had heard before but she could not recall the name. A smaller-sized piano sat in the center of the room. A small bookshelf was lined with thick volumes on the right side of the room. It had the feel of an old study. Turner grabbed a little remote from a table by an armchair, pointed it at the Bose, and turned the music down.

"That's a pretty piece," Kate said.

"One of my favorites," Turner said. "Bach's 'French Suite Number Six.'"

"It's actually because of your love for piano that we're here," Kate said.

"Oh yeah?"

"Yes. We're trying to find a man who is likely a piano tuner in the Frankfield and possibly the Chicago area. Knudsen said you had worked with one fairly recently."

"Well, I *called* one recently. He came over and worked on the piano and he did an okay job but to say he *worked* might be a stretch."

"What do you mean?"

"Well, he was a weird gentleman," Turner said. "He came in and I think all he said was *hello* before he went to the piano. He was here for about ten minutes, did his job, took my money, and left. Not sure why, but the whole thing sort of creeped me out."

"Any particular reason?"

"He barely acknowledged me at all. It was like he had punched a clock and stepped into some factory or something. He muttered to himself while he was tuning the piano. Not humming or anything like that, but actually muttering to himself. It reminded me of some of the homeless people you pass by from time to time up in the city. I know that might sound crude, but it's exactly the vibe I got from him."

"Did he seem menacing at all?"

"No…not really. But I did feel like I wanted him out of my house. He was like some sort of ghoul or something."

"Do you have a name and number?"

"His name was Eric Letterman. I'll have to dig for his number because I had no intention of ever using it again." He reached to the table by the armchair again and grabbed his cell phone. As he scrolled through his call history in the hopes of finding the number, Kate went on with the questioning.

"How did you learn about his services?"

"I don't remember, honestly. Maybe in the local paper? I think that's right, but I honestly don't remember. Maybe Facebook…"

"Had you heard of him before?"

"No, I don't believe so." He stopped scrolling and then showed the agents his phone. "Right here. Eric Letterman."

Kate moved to type the number down in her phone but, as usual, DeMarco was the quicker of them when it came to all things tech. She simply snapped a picture of Turner's screen and re-pocketed her phone. It took less than three seconds.

"Anything else you can tell us about him?" Kate asked. "Identifying marks, what he was driving, things like that?"

Turner thought about it for a moment before shaking his head. "I'm sorry, but no. The only thing I can tell you is that he was middle-aged. Maybe a little younger than me. Probably in his fifties. But that's all I've got. Like I said…we never spoke. He stayed in here and when it was clear that he was an antisocial type, I left him to it. Went into the kitchen and puttered around."

"Well, I think you've given us more than enough," Kate said, turning and heading for the door. "Thank you for your time."

"Sure," Turner said, walking with them to the door. He seemed a little perplexed, like a man in a whirlwind. The visit had lasted less than five minutes and he looked as if he almost regretted that his company was leaving so soon. "How is Knudsen doing anyway?" he asked. "I haven't spoken to him in about two months."

"He's ... grumpy," Kate said.

"So the same, in other words."

Turner gave them a wave and a smile as they headed down his porch steps and back across the shadow-covered front lawn. Kate looked over and saw that DeMarco was already saving Eric Letterman's number into her phone. By the time they made it to the car, she had already called Bannerman's men and was requesting an address.

Kate smiled in spite of the situation. DeMarco was going to be pretty much untouchable within a few years.

It's a good thing, too, she thought. *Because in about half an hour, Duran is going to be on to you and that could very well be the end of your second career.*

As it turned out, Eric Letterman lived only two miles away from the home of Marjorie and David Hix. It was a decrepit-looking house, tucked away on the corner of what Kate assumed was the so-called downtown area of Frankfield. A single black pickup truck sat on the curb in front of the house. The lawn was slightly overgrown and the columns on the porch could use a good sanding and coat of paint.

As they made their way toward the house, Kate peered into the back of the pickup truck. If it belonged to Eric Letterman, it appeared as if he might be a jack-of-all-trades. There was a tied down toolbox in the back, as well as a sledgehammer, a shovel, and two cinderblocks. None of the items was really enough to make her suspicious, but they certainly did not set her mind at ease, either.

She and DeMarco walked up onto the porch, where Kate knocked on the screen door. They were instantly met with the sound of a barking dog—a smaller breed from the sound of it. A man's groaning voice sounded out from somewhere in the house.

Kate could not make out the words, but she was pretty sure the voice was telling the dog to shut up.

They heard footfalls approaching, punctuated by the creaking of floorboards. The door was opened moments later by a man dressed in a dingy white T-shirt and jeans. It was clear that he had been interrupted from something. His forehead was coated in sweat and he looked irritated that he had been interrupted. A Jack Russell terrier ran laps around his feet, growling at the unexpected visitors on the porch.

"Hi," he said uncertainly.

"Hello," Kate said. "Are you Eric Letterman?"

"I am. And you are ...?"

She realized as she pulled her badge that this might very well be their guy. It made the act of reaching for her ID a little nerve-wracking. She could feel each moment ticking by, but slowly, as if she was moving through water.

"We're Agents Wise and DeMarco, with the FBI."

He eyed Kate's ID rather suspiciously but after a few seconds, a slow realization crept into his face. "I see. Is there something I can help you with?"

"Can we come inside?"

He shrugged, a little embarrassed. "You can, sure. But the place is a mess."

"That's quite all right."

Letterman invited them inside, picking things up along the way as he led them though his hall. It *was* a mess, though not nearly as bad as some other places Kate had seen. She watched carefully as he picked up after himself, making sure he wasn't trying to hide anything incriminating. She saw nothing to cause concern: a pair of shoes, an empty Amazon package, an empty soda bottle.

He led them into the living room, which smelled of lemon-scented polish. She saw a violin on a rack on the right side of the room. On the left, there was an ornate-looking harp—the sort that should be in a stage play rather than actually used.

"I see the instruments here," DeMarco said. "Are you a musician?"

"I used to be," he said. "But after a few failed attempts to make it onto the Chicago Symphony Orchestra, I called it quits. I've been tuning, repairing, and repurposing instruments ever since then."

"Is it what you do for a living?" Kate asked.

"More or less," he said, wiping his brow with a handkerchief he pulled from his back pocket. "I've got an old church organ out back in my little work area that I've been tinkering with for the better part of a week or so. But there's no way *just* this sort of stuff would pay the bills. I have a YouTube channel where I cover classic rock songs on violin, cello, and classical guitar. I also sell my stuff on Bandcamp online."

"Do you think we could see the organ you're working on?" Kate asked.

"Sure," he said, clearly surprised. "Come on back. But the house gets messier the further in we go."

"I assure you, that's quite all right," Kate said again.

Letterman led them through the house, all the way to the back and through his kitchen. The Jack Russell followed along, sniffing at Kate's and DeMarco's feet. Off of the kitchen, they walked into what was clearly a small built-on room. It was in nicer shape than the rest of the house, though quite small. There was indeed an old-looking church organ in the room. It was propped on its side, held steady with straps and a few makeshift sawhorses. The back of it had been opened up to reveal the inner workings.

"Do you enjoy what you do?" DeMarco asked.

"I do."

"And how many pianos would you say you tune in the space of a month?"

"It depends. I'm not exactly the best when it comes to marketing. So some months, I might tune three. Others, none."

"When was the last time you tuned a piano for a customer?"

He thought for a moment, folding his arms and looking to the inside of the organ. "Maybe three weeks ago."

"Who was the customer?"

"A guy named Dan Fritz. A single dad, brought this old clunker of a piano online for his daughter."

"Three weeks ago?"

He nodded.

"No pianos since then?"

He started to see where this was going and, as such, seemed to start to get defensive. It alarmed Kate a bit, but she did not sense that they were in danger.

"No pianos. I've tuned a fixer-upper-type cello since then, but that's it. Everything else has been maintenance work like this."

"Mr. Letterman, did you ever tune a piano for a gentleman named Barry Turner?"

"Yes, I did. That's been ... I don't know ... maybe six months ago, give or take."

"What about Karen Hopkins, Marjorie Hix, or Meredith Lowell?" DeMarco asked. "Did you ever work with any of them?"

"Marjorie Hix, yes. It's been a while but I do remember tuning her piano. A beautiful piano, too." He paused here and Kate could literally see the pieces clicking together in his head. "What's going on here?"

"Mr. Letterman, we'll get to the point. We're investigating a series of murders in the area and currently, everything points to the murderer being a piano tuner."

"Karen Hopkins ... yeah, I heard about her. I heard she had died ... but *killed*?"

"Yes, that's right."

"Marjorie Hix ... dead?"

"Yes. And while we obviously can't get into the details, your name came up."

Letterman looked as if he had been slapped hard across the face. He looked hard at both women, as if he were trying to determine if they were pulling a prank on him. When he realized that they were indeed serious, he started to shake his head. "No, no, not me. I would never even ... why would I even be considered?"

"A piano teacher who was linked to the case gave us a tip that eventually led to your name," Kate said. "As you might imagine, it was an easy leap; there aren't many piano tuners in the area, even when you get into the Chicago population."

Letterman started to look afraid and a little bewildered. Kate tried to gauge if the confusion in his eyes was genuine or if he was a very good actor, but she could not tell just yet.

"I don't see how I can be seen as potentially guilty just because of what I do for a living," he said.

"I understand that frustration. But with a very short list, we need to start where it makes the most sense. And since your name came up..."

"Mr. Letterman," DeMarco said, "do you know of any other tuners in the area?"

His eyes narrowed and then he slowly started to nod. "Sort of. I don't know that he's still doing it, but..."

"But what?" Kate asked.

Letterman sat down on a workbench next to the organ. He looked bothered about something—not worried about his own future, but as if he was quickly sorting through a series of thoughts that made no sense to him.

"When I stopped trying to play professionally, I knew I wanted to do something with music. I also had a love for fixing things, maybe even building things. So for a while, I toyed with buying these older models of pianos, guitars, and violins, and trying to fix them up. It was a labor of love and while it did make some money for me, it was a handful. So I took on an apprentice—this other guy that didn't quite make it with the orchestra. A guy named Darby Insbrook. Talented guy but just... well, one of those that tried to master everything, you know? He was too divided between his love of the cello and his love of the piano to ever really nail down one of them, you know? But we became friends and I looked him up when I turned my back on it all. I asked him if he wanted to sort of be an assistant with what I was doing, and he came on board for a while."

"I take it you don't work with him any longer?" Kate asked.

"No. It didn't last long. He … he was obsessed with the work. And he had an angry streak on him that I had not seen in practices and auditions."

"What kind of an angry streak?"

"He'd get drunk and want to fight anyone that dared to bring up his failures. He would also get quite graphic about his sexual exploits. That was what made me part ways with him. He was telling me how he had met this girl online … a young girl, like seventeen or eighteen. He got drunk one night and told me he sometimes had these fantasies …"

"Rape fantasies, you mean?" DeMarco asked.

"No clue," Letterman said. And when he looked up at Kate and looked into her eyes, she believed every word of what he was telling them. "He never really described them to me, but I could tell he wanted to. Honestly, he just creeped me right the hell out."

A chill rode down Kate's spine but she managed to get out her next question without wavering.

"Mr. Letterman … do you know where we might find Insbrook?"

Letterman gave his best guess through a series of his own tremors and tears, looking back into the guts of the church organ as if he wanted to hide there.

CHAPTER TWENTY TWO

When Anna Forester let him into her home, he did his best not to stare at her neck. She was fairly attractive, he supposed. She looked to be in her early fifties, though she had done her makeup in a way to try to make the world think she was much younger. Still, her smile was pleasant and, as was the case with all of them, she was apparently quite trusting.

The Forester house was a two-story farmhouse knock-off, with wooden beams on the porch and high ceilings inside. Anna led him past the foyer, down a spacious hallway where everything was brightly lit through the picture windows facing them from the kitchen. But before they reached the kitchen, she led him into a smaller room. There was a desk pushed against the far wall, complete with a laptop and a pretentious-looking lamp. She led him to the far corner of the room where a fairly standard Yamaha piano sat.

"There she is," Anna said. "She's been good but there are just too many keys out of tune now. I can't just ignore it. I've got a son that needs to start practicing for a recital in a few months and I promised him we'd get this taken care of."

"Shouldn't be a problem," he said. "Do you know right off hand which keys are out of tune?"

"Sorry... no. My husband could tell you, but he's at work."

"No worries. I'll see what I can get done and be out of your hair within half an hour to an hour or so. I'll grab my tarp out of the back of my truck to lay the tools on; I don't want to scratch up this gorgeous wooden floor."

"Perfect. If you need me, I'll be doing laundry. Laundry room is through the living room and down the hall off the left."

He gave an utterly cheesy "OK" sign by making a circle with his pointer finger and thumb. She gave him an obligatory grin before leaving the room. He watched her go, finally taking a moment to really look at her neck. For some men, he knew it was all about the breasts or the butt. However, he had always been fascinated by the neck of a woman, particularly the curve where it met the shoulder and the area just above the collarbone. Not that it aroused him in any way; he simply knew this was a vulnerable spot.

He waited until she was out of the room before he headed for the hallway and the front door beyond. He walked back out to his truck, sauntering down the sidewalk as if he belonged there. Because as far as anyone in the neighborhood knew, he *did* belong there.

He grabbed his toolbox and the old battered tarp out of the back of his truck. He did know how to tune a piano and when he truly was on *actual* jobs where he had no ulterior motives, he was damned good at it. So, when he walked back toward the house with his tools in hand, he did so with a confident step. He looked around at the lush green yard and the neighboring yard as well, separated only by a large, towering oak. No cars in the driveway and the garage was closed. Of course, that meant nothing on the surface, but it was a good indication that there was likely no one home.

He walked back into the Forester house and went directly back to the piano. He set his things down carefully, knowing that any evidence he left behind in terms of the piano itself would end up in and on the tarp and carried out of the house, just as he had done with the first three women in Frankfield.

He tried to remember just how many times he had done this, but each occurrence sort of blurred with the next.

As he lifted the cover of the piano to expose the keys beneath, he heard Anne's soft footfalls in the kitchen. A cabinet opened. A glass clinked on the counter. Something was poured into it.

"How long has your son been playing?" he called out.

"About a year. The teacher at his school says he's got an exceptional talent for it. He's only eleven but can play at the level of kids that go to college for it. She says he might end up being some sort of prodigy or something."

He smiled to hear that she had no real issues engaging in conversation. "That's exciting," he said. "Already looking into scholarships?"

She surprised him when she came to the entryway between the office and the kitchen. She leaned against the doorframe and smiled. "His teacher has started gathering up some things, yeah. It really is exciting. Did you once play?"

"Once, yes. I still do from time to time, but I think I lost the drive. I'm perfectly happy to just fix up problem pianos these days, though."

"Well, I'm just glad you could make it out as soon as you did. I called some place in Chicago and they couldn't get out here until the end of the week. And my kiddo is *dying* to start playing."

"Is he your only one?"

"No. I've got another one, all grown up and married. I'm actually headed out of town next week because she's due with her first baby *any day* now. My first grandchild. Whew... that's hard to say."

He chuckled because, quite frankly, he was done with small talk. To get the point across, he started to push down the keys, one by one, with determined purpose. He cocked his ear to listen and nodded. He then took his tuner out of the toolbox—a device he had hardly ever used but had managed to pull off as a great disguise of sorts many times. Seeing it, Anna gave a polite little smile and walked out of his sight—presumably to do laundry as she had mentioned earlier.

He knew he needed to act quickly. If she was a chatty one and kept coming back, it was going to make his *real* intention here much harder.

It's got to be now, he thought. *She needs to be dead in the next two minutes.*

He went ahead and packed back up the tools he had taken out so far. The time for pretending was over. He tidied up so he would not have to do it afterward and then ran his fingers almost sensually along the keys. He came to the one he was most interested in—the D from the middle scale—and plinked it. The note was mostly in tune; had he actually been here to tune the piano, it would be a string he'd certainly adjust.

But that was not why he was here. Instead of fixing it, he set to removing the string completely—so he could include it in his own creation, waiting back at home for him in his workshop.

CHAPTER TWENTY THREE

Kate had been wrong. Duran had given her until nearly two o'clock before he started to call for her. The first call came at 1:46, as she and DeMarco were rushing to the address Eric Letterman had given them. She ignored it right away. When she did, DeMarco gave her a discerning eye from behind the wheel.

"You may as well answer it. This close to having a very likely suspect, I very seriously doubt he's going to bring the hammer down so hard."

Kate knew DeMarco was right, but she was far too focused right now. The last thing she wanted to do was to storm in after their first truly strong suspect with whatever choice words Duran had for her ringing in her ears. She did pick the phone back up but instead of returning Duran's call, she pulled up Bannerman's number. They had spoken just three minutes before so when he answered, there was excitement in his voice.

"You already there?" he asked.

"No. Still about five minutes out. I was wondering if you could send at least one unit over as backup, just in case. We know this guy has no issue killing women and that he's quite crafty about it. I don't see him overpowering us, but I *can* see him having some sort of escape plan ready for instances like these."

"Seems like I'm a mind reader," Bannerman said. "I sent a unit that way right after I got off the phone with you before. If you're five minutes out, he should be coming in right behind you."

"Make sure we're there before he stops. I don't want to give ourselves away before we even get there."

"Roger that," Bannerman said and ended the call.

The moment Kate set the phone down in her lap, it rang again. She checked the display and saw that it was Duran again. She sighed, looked to DeMarco with a worried grin, and then answered it.

"Kate, where are you?"

She knew he was pissed because he used her first name rather than calling her *Wise*. "I'm currently in pursuit."

"Of what, exactly?" he said, nearly hissing.

"A potential suspect. A *likely* suspect."

"And why the hell aren't you home like you're supposed to be?"

"Because it would be much harder to catch this suspect from home, sir."

He uttered a profanity, something she had not heard him do very much during their twenty-plus years of working together. "You're disobeying a direct order from your superior," he said, still in that hiss-like voice. "Do you understand what that could do to you and your otherwise stellar record?"

"I do, sir. And with all due respect, we're about two minutes out from an arrest. So you can tell me all about that when we're done."

The silence on the phone was heavy and felt as if there was a sharp edge to it. She was waiting for him to threaten her, to perhaps tell her that when she got home, they would terminate the contract they had between them. But in the end, he simply said: "Finish there. The moment you get back to DC, bring your ass to my office."

"Understood, sir." And with that, she hung up.

"You know," DeMarco said, "he's going to go off on me, too. I was supposed to tell on you if you didn't go back after he ordered you to."

"Why didn't you?"

DeMarco shrugged. "Because you don't need a babysitter."

"Thank you, DeMarco."

She worried what consequences DeMarco would have to pay for her part in this. But those thoughts did not have much time to gain traction, as DeMarco slowed the car to a crawl as they approached Darby Insbrook's residence.

The timing could not have been better. As DeMarco parked, they saw a Frankfield PD car cruise by the end of the block and then turn in their direction. It slowed down as DeMarco pulled their car to the curb. The police car cruised by, the driver eyeing the agents as they stepped out of the car, and then continued to the end of the block where he finally stopped and parked.

Having gotten the conversation with Duran out of the way, Kate was able to approach Insbrook's front door with a bit of confidence. Sure, she knew there were repercussions on the way but for now, she could simply be an agent. She could go in and get the job done knowing that, more or less, she had permission to do so. She would face the consequences later.

She knocked on the door and waited. She exchanged a tense look with DeMarco as they waited for an answer and got none. She had shared glances like this in the past, chalking them up to some sort of almost telepathic ability between people who are putting their lives on the line at the same time, people who are relying on one another for protection.

The thought that seemed to bounced between their minds was one of assurance—one of danger, too.

This is it. We're here. This is the end…

Kate knocked again, realizing that every muscle in her body seemed to be on edge, waiting for something to happen. When she was met with only silence again, she looked to DeMarco, hoping for another of those borderline supernatural pushes, but there was nothing.

She tried the door and was not surprised to find it locked. Kate knew that protocol told them to wait until Insbrook got back home. But Kate had overridden protocol with good old intuition numerous times in her career and her intuition had been right far more often than not.

"Let's see if there's a back door," Kate said.

DeMarco nodded her agreement and started down the porch steps ahead of Kate. One behind the other, they sprinted to the back of the house. Kate did not feel at all odd about putting speed into her step. She could still feel that certainty she had felt on the porch—a certainty that seemed to grow with the passing of each minute.

At the back of the house, the yard had gone to pot. The grass was tall and dead in some places. A few dead rose bushes clung to the side of the house and scattered pieces of wood. Kate saw the ruins of an old piano, the legs dismantled and the grayed keys seeming to smile at her. Beside all of this there was a small set of stairs that led to a back door. DeMarco climbed the stairs and tried the door, finding it locked as well.

DeMarco frowned and looked back down to Kate, standing in the overgrown yard.

"Hey, remember how I didn't turn you in to Duran when you failed to go back home when he asked?" DeMarco asked.

"Yeah," Kate said, confused.

"Good. If you keep *this* to yourself, I think we can call it even."

Before Kate could ask any questions, DeMarco took one lunging step back and then delivered a solid kick into the door. The wood splintered and the door buckled, but it did not give. With another grunt and a stronger kick from DeMarco, the hinges popped off and clattered to the ground, barely audible over the commotion the door made as it flew inward.

Kate was glad DeMarco had done it. Kate herself had been on the verge of wanting to do the exact same thing at the front door.

Kate fell in behind DeMarco and they entered the house. Right away, Kate took in the smells of old wood, some sort of polish or enamel, and an overall workshop sort of smell. The back door opened up onto a sparse kitchen that held a strong odor of black coffee—barely noticeable over the smell of wood and polish.

They exited the kitchen and entered a hallway that seemed to extend most of the length of the house. They passed by a small bedroom on the right, which DeMarco split off into. Kate fell in behind, saw the room was small and unoccupied, and continued down the hall. A doorway appeared on her right, partially open. She peered into the crack between the wall and the frame. A wooden staircase led down into a dark area. The woodshop smell seemed to come from the darkness below. Kate hit the light switch on the wall just inside the doorway and peered down the stairway. A dingy basement floor waited at the bottom of the stairs.

"I think I've found the workshop," Kate called out.

"Kate…"

Kate paused and watched DeMarco come out of the bedroom. She held something in her hand that made no sense at first. But then it registered and it felt like ice forming in Kate's veins.

DeMarco was holding a decapitated Barbie doll. Its entire nude body was wrapped in old piano string.

"Jesus…" Kate whispered.

As DeMarco neared her and they looked down into the basement, they both drew their weapons.

"If anyone is home, I need you to come out and make yourself known," Kate said. But her voice had fallen on enough empty homes in the past for her to know they were alone in the house. Still, it made it no easier to descend the basement stairs without knowing what awaited them below.

At the bottom of the stairs, Kate took a moment to take it all in. She found herself standing in front of a makeshift aisle that ran between two rows of junked pianos. It reminded her of those shows like *American Pickers* where people scavenged old sheds and houses for hidden treasures. Kate didn't know enough about pianos to know if any of these gutted pianos were treasures or not, but it was certainly interesting.

And a little creepy, if she was being honest.

"What the hell is all of this?" DeMarco asked as they made their way down the little aisle.

"His projects, I suppose. If he was tuning pianos, maybe he's reclaiming them, too. Sort of like Barry Turner."

"Maybe he's been collecting piano wire for them…"

Kate had been thinking the same thing but the idea of speaking it out loud had seemed almost like a bad omen. Still, she sauntered forward, her eyes on the piano at the end of the row on her left. The top was opened and covered by a tarp. It seemed to be the only one of the piano bodies that had been touched as of late.

When she reached out for the tarp to pull it back, her mind's eye pulled up several terrible images, preparing itself for the worst. When she saw nothing but piano wire and small fragments of dust inside, she was shocked.

DeMarco fell in beside her and when she did, Kate started to understand what she was seeing. She hoped to God she was jumping to conclusions but something inside of her—a part of her that had seen the worst in people, sometimes down to what she would call absolute evil—knew better.

The piano was missing many strings. She recalled from her brief introduction to the piano as a child that a piano had eighty-eight keys and more than two hundred strings inside. While this piano was far away from having all of its strings, the number she saw was alarming.

Not because of the number... but because each wire installed inside the body of it contained a single strand of hair.

"Twenty-three," DeMarco said.

"What?"

"Twenty-three strings."

"You see the hairs?"

"I wish I didn't. Do you think they're all from the three women in Frankfield?"

"I hope that's the case," Kate said. "My fear is that each hair is from a different victim."

"But... twenty-three..."

The idea hung in the air like some poisonous chemical, making it hard to move. Kate backed away slowly, getting her speed and breath bit by bit with each step. By the time she got to the stairs, she was nearly running.

"Where are you going?" DeMarco called, still frozen by the piano and its secrets.

"We have to figure out where he is."

"How?"

But Kate was already up the stairs and barely heard the question. She dashed into the bedroom DeMarco had already checked but found it useless—though there was another wired Barbie in the floor. When she ran out of the room and toward what she assumed would be the living room area, she nearly collided with DeMarco as she came out of the basement.

Twenty-three, Kate thought as she hurried into the living room. *Twenty-three strings, twenty-three hairs… God, please don't let my hunch be right… please…*

She entered the living room and found it oddly neat. There was a single recliner and a loveseat, a coffee table, and a flat-screen TV sitting on a low entertainment center. There was an address book on the coffee table, and a wireless landline phone sitting on a small end table by the love seat.

Kate scooped up the address book, knocking off a few magazines in the process—*Guitar Magazine, Orchestral, Entertainment Weekly.* She thumbed through the address book, stopping at the H section. Little jolts of electricity coursed through her when she saw listings for *Hopkins, Karen* and *Hix, Marjorie.* Their addressee were written beneath the names in a very neat handwriting. There were two more names on the H pages but they were not local. One was from Winston-Salem, North Carolina. Another was from Engle, Ohio.

"Oh my God," Kate said, as she started to understand that perhaps she *had* been right.

Twenty-three…

She handed DeMarco the book, letting her come to her own conclusions. When she did, a folded piece of notebook paper partially slid out of the back cover. Kate took it, unfolded it, and saw several names. Three were familiar: Karen Hopkins, Marjorie Hix, Meredith Lowell.

They were all crossed out. Above their names, two others were crossed out in harsh red marks.

The next name on the list was Anna Forester. Her number was beside it.

Kate wasted no time. She pulled out her cell phone and called the number. Even as the phone started to ring, her gut tightened as she was somehow certain no one would answer. And then another number started barreling through her head, one that made her feel sick.

Twenty-four...

CHAPTER TWENTY FOUR

Anna Forester was folding her husband's jeans when it occurred to her that in about a week or so, her daughter would be folding little onesies. Anna could barely remember what it was like to wash those tiny little baby clothes and part of her badly missed it. She decided right then and there that she was going to be one of those grandmothers who spoiled the absolute hell out of her grandchildren.

As she set the jeans on her husband's pile of clothes and reached for one of her blouses, the piano tuner spoke up from the other room. Anna supposed it was her fault; she had been overly chatty at first and now he seemed to not want to shut up.

"They got any names picked out for your grandchild?"

"None yet," she answered, having to raise her voice to a near shout to be heard from the laundry room. She had no idea why, but there was something off-putting about the fact that he was yelling at her from elsewhere in the house, even if it was to ask random questions. It almost seemed as if he was trying to make sure he always knew where she was.

"A boy or girl?" he asked.

She rolled her eyes, now good and tired of having this conversation in a borderline shouting match. "They want to be surprised!"

"Aww, that's nice," he responded.

Was it just her imagination, or did he sound closer now? She cocked her head, curious and a little upset. Was he seriously moving through her house? Was he some sort of thief? Was he some sort of—

Her thought was interrupted by the ringing of her phone. Her ring tone was the little catchy scale in Bob Marley's "Three Little Birds," a reminder not to get pissed off when unexpected phone calls interrupted her day.

She reached for her back pocket as she stepped out of the laundry room. As she entered the kitchen, she pulled the phone from her pocket and was very confused for a moment. This made no sense. The name on the caller ID was something she had put in just a few days ago. It read: Piano Tuner Guy.

"Umm…" she said into the kitchen.

She was weirded out to the point of being a little scared. Was he actually calling from inside the house? She could hear him moving around in the office, probably thinking of some other question to ask. Instead of walking out to see what was going on, she remained in the kitchen and answered the call. As she did, some primal part of her brain kicked in and she reached for the laundry room door handle.

She answered the call. "Hello?"

"Anna Forester?" a woman asked. She sounded hurried and a little frightened.

"Y…Yes. Who is this?" Fear clutched at her heart until she found it hard to breathe. Something was very wrong; it was a realization that started to settle in on her like drying cement.

"I need you to remain calm as I reveal this information to you and as I ask you some questions. I'm Kate Wise, an FBI agent here in Frankfield. With a simple yes or no, I need you to tell me if there is currently a man in your home that is there to tune a piano."

The dread tightened around her heart and she felt the need to scream. She fought it back, though, and let out a croaky-sounding "Yes."

"Are you in the same room with him?"

"No."

"Good. Get somewhere where you can close a door between the two of you."

"What is—"

"Just do as I say. I'll tell you what I can as you move."

"Okay…"

But just as she said that, the tuner appeared in the entryway to the kitchen. It was almost as if he knew the phone call was about him. He regarded her with a bit if suspicion, no doubt alerted by the look of terror on her face. He took a single step into the kitchen, the stern look on his face an indication that he knew something was up. He held a single length of piano wire in his hands, holding it like a piece of rope he was about to tie into a knot.

"Get into another room and close the door," the agent said in her ear, though her voice sounded as if it was a million miles away.

Anna realized then that no matter which way she went, the tuner could easily cut her off. The kitchen island sat in the center of the room, the only thing between them. If she went to the left, toward the laundry room, he could easily cut her off. If she ran to the right, there was the hallway and three rooms to choose from: the master bedroom, the powder room, and the guest room.

"Are you okay?" the agent asked in her ear.

"No." It came out shaky. As if she were a wounded lamb, the tuner took another step forward. The smile on his face spoke of his intentions and suddenly, Anna wondered if she would ever get to meet her grandchild at all.

Knowing that she had to move quickly, she started left, acting as if she was heading for the laundry room. The tuner bit hard and started in that direction, too. When she saw him moving, Anna reversed direction and headed to the right. She sprinted out of the kitchen and into the hallway. She heard the tuner let out a curse behind her and then the sound of him slamming into the kitchen island as he quickly changed course.

"Ms. Forester, are you okay?"

"He's coming after me," she squeaked, headed for the bedroom.

"Okay, you close the door and lock it. I'm on my way. Maybe two or three minutes. If you can—"

That was the last thing Anna heard. As she entered the bedroom and turned to shut the door, the piano tuner was there. He reached out and grabbed her by the shoulder. Anna reached out to slap his hand away but he blocked it easily. He frowned a bit as he darted out his right hand in an inexperienced punch. It caught her in the jaw and Anne's head rocked back. As it did, the man reached out and grabbed her hair. He pulled her to him with such force that her feet came off of the ground. Her scalp felt like someone had set it on fire.

She screamed, dropping the phone to the floor. She watched it dumbly, as if through someone else's eyes, while the piano tuner wrenched her around and trapped her neck in the crook of his arm. She fought against it and, for just a moment, thought she had managed to free herself.

But the pressure of his arm was replaced by something else—some thinner pressure that seemed to lightly sink into her flesh. She tried to scream but found that she could not get much of anything through her throat—just a little squeak of terror.

She started to choke right there in the doorway of her bedroom. She felt him trying to pull her back slightly, pulling her feet off of the floor. She knew if he succeeded, that was the end of it. She'd be dead. She flailed, feeling the wire around her neck tighten. She did her best to stay calm, but dread was flooding her mind. Somewhere in the flood there was the smallest little speck of reason, and it told her that she had only one chance to escape this. He was pulling slightly up still, but not *back*. The tuner seemed perfectly fine to strangle her right there in her doorway.

And that was the single mistake he had made. Anna, still flailing, kicked her right foot out and found the doorframe. She then kicked away from it, putting every bit of strength she had into it. It wasn't very hard, but it was enough to cause the tuner to lose his balance just slightly. As he tried to compensate, Anna brought her knees up, allowing her weight to sag down. For just an instant, the tightness around her throat was immense but the tactic caught the tuner off guard. This displaced weight caused him to stumble forward. As he did, he lost his grip on her.

Anna knew she should probably lash out or attack or something...but the call from the FBI agent had clued her in to how dangerous this man could be—as if his attempt to strangle her just now had not been enough. So the moment Anna was free, she ran.

She darted toward the kitchen, intending to hit the back door, go down the back porch steps and to her neighbor's house. Her phone was on the floor in the bedroom and while they *did* have a gun in the house, it was in a safe in the top of her closet—directly behind the would-be killer.

So she ran for the kitchen. She made it three strides down the hallway before she felt his weight slam into her back. Anna went sailing forward, catching herself on the island in the kitchen. Pinned between the tuner and the island, she felt an explosion of pain radiate through her chest. Undaunted, she grabbed for the drawer to her right, over the ledge of the island's counter. In doing so, she knocked the cup of coffee she had been drinking from the island. It shattered on the floor, and lukewarm coffee soaked her left pants leg.

She had struck the island so hard that the tuner had bounced slightly off of her, equally jarred by the impact. This allowed her a split second to reach into the drawer she had managed to open, looking for the butcher's knife. In the back of her head, she reminded herself that the stupid thing was dull; it was a complaint she made every time she used it, hoping her husband would show some initiative and sharpen it.

But as her hand fell on the handle, she figured it she stabbed hard enough, it would surely sink in. All she had to do was—

He grabbed the arm reaching for the knife and twisted it hard. She tried to wrench it away but he pulled her to him. As she slammed into his chest and he tried to wrap an arm around her again, she desperately threw her right hand out, clenched in a small fist. It landed right across his brow, not hard, but unexpected. He blinked as if he was trying to dislodge something from his eye as Anna yanked her arm free and ran for the back door.

He was on to her, though. He leaped up on the island and slid across it, nearly falling off. He had cut off her escape route, sensing what she had planned. With a scream, Anna ran for the laundry room at the far end of the kitchen.

She knew he was on her heels but if she could just get to the laundry room and close the door, maybe she could hold him off until the FBI got there.

She made it to the doorway, the smell of laundry detergent and dryer sheets sweeter than ever before. She entered the room and turned to shut the door, but he was already there, standing in the doorway. When she tried slamming the door in his face anyway, he simply batted it aside.

Anna tried to fight against him as he came in, but with nowhere left to go, she was easy prey. As he pushed her hard against the wall, all Anna could do was wonder what in the hell was taking that FBI woman so long.

CHAPTER TWENTY FIVE

When DeMarco slammed on the brakes in front of the Forester home, Kate was nearly thrown directly into the dashboard despite the seatbelt. DeMarco threw the car into park and both women got out, sprinting directly to the front door. Kate was not at all surprised to find it locked and started to draw her foot back to kick it in. She then saw that the lock beneath the knob was an electronic one and decided she'd rather not dislocate her ankle or knee.

"Stand back," DeMarco said, leveling her gun toward the lock.

Kate swiveled to the side and winced as DeMarco fired off a single shot. The lock was obliterated and made a series of clicking noises. DeMarco drew back and delivered a harsh kick that sent the door flying inward, her second such attack of the day.

Kate flanked in, ducking down with her gun drawn, as DeMarco came in behind her. Right away, they could hear the sounds of struggle. It sounded as if it was coming from the very back of the house. Kate and DeMarco nodded to one another and headed forward, not bothering to be stealthy, as the gunshot to the front door had very likely ruined their cover.

As they came to the end of the hallway, the signs of a struggle were evident: a picture was knocked from the hallway wall; a coffee mug had been shattered on the floor, its contents splashed on the tile; several drawers were opened and silverware littered the floor around the edges of the kitchen bar.

A choking sound followed by a hollow thudding noise came from further back behind the kitchen. Kate sprinted forward, into what looked like a mudroom. To the right, there was a partially opened door. From inside, there was a commotion, a tangle of bodies and the wretched sounds of someone choking.

"FBI!"

Kate screamed this as she drew up her gun and kicked the door open fully with her foot. The door, though, would not swing all the way open. It was stopped by one of the bodies on the floor. It was a man, kneeling over a woman Kate assumed to be Anna Forester.

And the man, she assumed, was Darby Insbrook.

"Get off of her," Kate said, not quite in a yell but in a voice that had some ice to it.

The tuner responded in a way that made no sense to Kate at first. He swung his head around and did, in fact, look to be obeying. But as he started to stand, his right foot kicked out at the door and it came rushing back in Kate's direction. She blocked it easily but when it stopped, he was there.

Insbrook swung hard, his right hand connecting with Kate's cheek. She tumbled back directly into DeMarco. Both women stumbled backward, Kate doing everything she could to stay on her feet. DeMarco, on the other hand, hit the mudroom wall and rebounded hard. She tried raising her gun to fend off Insbrook, but he already had the door closed again.

Kate acted without thinking. She charged at the door, slamming her entire weight into it. It caught Insbrook off guard and sent him sprawling back. His feet tangled over Anna Forester's body and he barely caught himself on the edge of the dryer. A pile of folded clothes went toppling over into the floor. In the back of her mind, Kate heard herself laughing maniacally. So far, this was easily the clumsiest fight she had ever been in.

He pushed himself off of the dryer and launched himself at her. Kate fired off a round but it was at the same moment she slammed into her. The bullet tore into the wall just a foot or so behind Insbrook's head. It was not a shoulder thrown into her chest or even a punch or kick. Their bodies simply slammed together. He felt as if he easily had fifty or more pounds on her, and the result was nasty. Kate's forehead dinged off of the killer's chin and his knee slammed into her hip. They fell in a heap, the back of Kate's head striking the door frame of the laundry room. White sparks rocketed across her field of vision as something like dull electricity seemed to sweep across her head. She was dimly aware that somewhere in the melee, she had dropped her gun.

She was momentarily so blindsided and disoriented that she was barely aware that Insbrook kept going. He plowed through her and continued on. The only thing that brought Kate out of her stupor was the sound of another gunshot. There was a brief yelp of pain and then the sound of something thudding hard against the floor.

Kate scrambled to her hands and knees, fully expecting to see Darby Insbrook on the tile floor of the mudroom with DeMarco holding her Glock. Instead, the killer had DeMarco pinned to the wall—an elbow in her chest as he started to wrap a piece of piano wire around her neck with the other hand.

Kate tried getting to her feet, using the doorframe to help. The white sparks were still streaking across her line of vision and her knees felt incredibly shaky. Still, she hobbled forward and brought a knee up hard into Insbrook's side, aiming for his ribs. She nearly fell again, almost losing her balance and only able to stay on her feet by throwing her arms around Insbrook's neck. She did her best to maneuver it into a head lock but she was too weakened from the earlier blow. The important thing, though, was that Insbrook was off of DeMarco, trying to wriggle out of Kate's grasp.

He dropped to his knees slowly, reached back, and grabbed a handful of Kate's hair. She knew what was coming next and did her best to brace her feet against the mudroom wall to stop it. The killer hunched over in a kneeling U-posture, pulled her hair hard, and sent her sailing over his shoulder. Kate landed hard on her back and slid across the mudroom floor, into the kitchen. The breath went sailing out of her and the pain in her back caused her to curl into the fetal position. If she could have drawn in a breath, she would have let out a scream.

Insbrook came at her again, the piano wire still in his hand. She saw rage in his eyes, a dark glittering star that had no core. There was animalistic hatred there, an urge to hurt and maim and kill.

Kate saw the litter of silverware on the floor from the apparent struggle between Anna Forester and Darby Insbrook before she and DeMarco had arrived. She reached for a steak knife, her back screaming in pain as she did so. Even as she grasped for it, she knew she would be too late anyway.

The killer dove for her, the piano wire stretched out tightly between his hands. She had a moment to think of Karen Hopkins and how the wire had actually cut into her skin. She wondered if he could actually saw through her neck if he tried.

She raised the knife up and for the briefest of moments, there was hesitation. This was followed by what sounded like a strange snapping noise, organic and metallic sounding all at once. Insbrook howled—not a sound of pain, but of rage. Kate realized that when she had drawn the knife up, she had snapped the piano wire Insbrook had been wielding. She had snapped it right in half.

From the floor, Insbrook threw a hard elbow out toward her. It missed, but he followed with a lazy kick. This one caught her in the shin and though it did not hurt all that bad, she knew it was going to leave one hell of a bruise.

He came at her again and Kate managed to get to her knees before he could attack. She readied the knife, knowing that it was either him or her. If she did not cut him where it mattered, he might very well kill her.

But just before he struck her, there were two loud popping noises, a wet splash against Kate's chest, and then an unexpected right-handed veer to Insbrook's approach. He tottered hard to the right and collapsed onto the kitchen floor.

There was a hole in his forehead and another just below his neck. Both were dribbling out blood, the one beneath his neck pouring it out onto the floor. Kate looked behind where the killer had been coming from and saw DeMarco. She was still in her shooter's stance, her face like granite and her knuckles white as they gripped the Glock.

It occurred to Kate in that moment, as she saw the absolute shock and hatred on her partner's face, that DeMarco had not even tried to shoot to wound. Either of the shots could have been fatal, much less both.

"DeMarco... at ease. Okay?"

DeMarco only blinked once. Several spooky moments passed before DeMarco got to her feet. Kate did the same, leaning back against the kitchen bar as she realized she was still quite dizzy. Slowly, she walked over to DeMarco just as DeMarco seemed to slowly start to come around. They both looked back into the laundry room. Anna Forester was lying on the floor. As Kate walked slowly into the room, she prayed the woman was still alive.

Anna's eyes were open, staring up at the ceiling. At first Kate feared the woman was dead, but then she blinked. And then she started to cry.

Kate tried to kneel on the floor with her but ended up partially collapsing instead. She took the woman's hand in her own and did her best to remain rational.

"You're okay now," Kate said. "You're okay."

DeMarco watched on as she pulled her phone out and placed a call to Bannerman. Even as she spoke to him, filling him in on what happened, it was obvious that she was doing everything she could to hold back tears—and to not turn around to face the death she had just doled out.

CHAPTER TWENTY SIX

As the evening rolled on, Kate noticed that Sheriff Bannerman looked like he was in shock. He worked well and managed to keep his head above the water, but Kate knew the look on his face very well. She was pretty sure that when he got home that night, he was going to think long and hard about the years he had served as a sheriff and what his retirement might look like.

Kate did not get a chance to really speak to him until the ambulance had left the Forester house with Anna inside. As far as they could tell from first glance, she was going to have some massive bruising around her neck and she was in a serious state of shock. But all in all, Anna Forester was going to turn out okay.

When the ambulance left and the last of the patrol cars left behind it, Bannerman went to the porch swing on the Foresters' porch and sat down with a heavy sound that was part grunt and part sigh.

"You okay?" Kate asked.

"I will be. What about you? You got banged up pretty good. Don't think I haven't noticed that bruise on the side of your head."

"I'll be okay."

"I'll make her see a doctor," DeMarco said from the place where she was sitting on the stairs.

"So ... tell me about this piano I'm going to have to deal with," Bannerman said.

"You won't have to deal with it," DeMarco said. "We spoke with our supervisor and he's sending a special forensics team to look at it. There are hairs on those strings that could be a year or so old. And not from this area."

"So what does that mean? That he's done this before?"

"It looks that way," Kate said, still unable to believe it. "But we won't know for certain until the names we found in his address book are cross-examined with unexplained murders or disappearances over the last few years. And then we'll have to wait on the forensics details from those hair samples."

"But...?"

"But it feels like we just stopped a serial killer," DeMarco said.

Bannerman looked at Kate for some sort of confirmation and she nodded. He said nothing for a while and then got to his feet, though it was clear he was more than done for that day.

"Thank you, ladies, for all you've done. I guess I'll call a press conference of my own and let the locals know that the murders have come to a stop and the suspect has been killed." He looked at Kate and gave a knowing grin. "You sure you don't want to stick around for that?"

"Oh, I'm certain. But thanks anyway."

The three of them remained on the porch for a while longer. Kate did her best to hide the fact that her head was still reeling and she felt slightly sick to her stomach. She figured she'd have to get okayed by a doctor to fly back out to Virginia. She was all but certain she had a concussion.

But it had been worth it because it would be much easier to live the rest of her life constantly seeing the number *twenty-three* in her mind instead of *twenty-four*.

Because she did indeed have a concussion, Kate was unable to make the return trip back east for another twenty hours. She skipped going back home right away because she knew there would be her own drama to wrap up there—not only with Melissa, but with Alan as well. She flew direct from O'Hare to Dulles exactly twenty-one hours after saving Anne Forester's life.

She arrived back in DC with an email waiting for her. It was not from Duran's personal assistant, but from Duran himself. He would be in his office, waiting for her arrival. He also gave her a heads-up that the section chief may be in attendance.

Kate knew she should be worried but as she watched DC's early night traffic roll by through the windows of her cab, she felt a certain sense of peace to the whole thing. Yes, she knew it was not normal for Duran to hold meetings with agents at 8:30 at night. And she also knew that if the section chief—a wiry grunt of a man named Sam Hilton—was going to be in attendance, the meeting would likely have a very bad outcome.

It wasn't until she reached FBI headquarters that she realized why she wasn't stressed out over the meeting. Perhaps it was the high of taking out Darby Insbrook or just because she was tired, but she was starting to fully understand how blessed she was. She had been graced with a second chapter of a career she had loved *and* she had a daughter who loved her, despite her any flaws and stubborn tendencies. And, if she played her cards right, she even still had a salvageable relationship with a man who seemed to be very much in love with her despite her insistence on keeping him at arm's length.

In other words, no matter how the meeting turned out, she still had an amazing life waiting for her no matter the turns.

She took the elevator to the second floor after checking in with the after-hours guard. When the elevator dinged and the doors slid open, she walked to Duran's office with confidence in her step. It did waver a bit when she found the door already open, as if he was not only expecting her but wanted her to know that they were waiting specifically for her.

She entered the room and saw that Section Chief Hilton was indeed there. She'd only met with the man a handful of times during the course of her career and they had a good working relationship. Now, though, as he looked up from the small conference room table in the back of Duran's office, he gazed at her as if he was inspecting a bothersome insect that had been buzzing around his head.

Duran also sat at the table with him, but he got to his feet when Kate entered the room. It was an awkward sort of greeting that Duran seemed to regret instantly. He recovered as best as he could by simply pointing to one of the available chairs.

"Have a seat, Agent Wise," he said.

She did as she was asked, nodding to the section chief as she did so. "Section Chief Hilton, it's nice to see you."

"You as well. I do wish it was under better circumstances, though."

"What *are* the circumstances?" Kate asked.

Duran leaned forward a bit, as if to make sure he was not forgotten. "Well, once again we find ourselves torn over how to proceed with using you. As you remember, it was supposed to be only on rare occasions but this latest case—this discovery of Insbrook at work outside of Chicago—there's no way we're going to be able to ignore it. The media is going to latch on to it."

"Thanks in part," Hilton added, "to the little stunt you pulled at the press conference."

"I don't follow," Kate said.

Duran and Hilton shared an uncomfortable glance, but Duran eventually answered her. "The cross-checking of names is done. Each one of the names in the address book you found that had been crossed out...they're all homicides. Two were speculated to have been suicides but there was never enough evidence. They had all been strangled, but only several of the more recent ones had been strangled with what does now appear to have been piano wire. And while there have not been conclusive tests run on all of the hairs, there have been enough positive matches to these deceased women to be able to finish connecting the dots."

"Twenty-three, right?" she asked, the word seeming much larger than it actually was.

"Yes. If we count the three victims in Frankfield, there were twenty-three victims. And you stopped him. Twenty murders before he stepped foot in Frankfield and he somehow went unnoticed. Chief Hilton and I will be putting together a task force tomorrow to figure out how the hell he wasn't linked to these other twenty murders—murders that span back four years."

"So yes," Hilton said, "we acknowledge that you and Agent DeMarco took down a man that had killed twenty-three women. And *that* is the part the media is going to see and no doubt be talking about. But what they *won't* see or hear is how you willfully disobeyed your director's orders and essentially went rogue. Would you care to tell us why you thought you could just go about and do as you pleased?"

"I knew we were getting close," she said. "If I had left, it would have altered the progress of the case."

"You feel that highly about yourself?" Hilton asked.

"No, sir. But I have worked more than one hundred cases involving killers or suspected killers. I know enough about the structure of a case to know that once progress towards a solution begins, changing the personnel almost always slows the progress. Had we still been at square one with no leads at all, I would not have made that call."

"It wasn't your call to make, Kate," Duran said. He then looked to Hilton with a dash of embarrassment, realizing he had used her first name, showing a bit of favoritism and familiarity.

"Here's where we're at," Hilton said. "Director Duran and I have been going back and forth on it all day. Given the nature of your current agreement with the bureau, it would seem the most reasonable thing to do is call out your fault in disobedience and terminate the agreement. About three hours ago, we had come to that agreement. But then we saw that the news has already picked up on how a serial killer was stopped. Anna Forester gave the bit of testimony she has, and Sheriff Bannerman is going on and on about you and DeMarco. Throw in the fact that a few stations and websites are running your interference at that press conference on a loop, and you're connected to the case and the killer."

"But DeMarco deserves that credit. She's the one that took him down."

"We already spoke with her," Hilton said. "She insists you saved her life before she was able to shoot Insbrook. She said it was very much a team effort. And quite honestly, she's smart as hell; she does not want the credit or the recognition for taking out Insbrook. That much media and publicity for an agent so young... it could end up spoiling her career."

Kate nodded, feeling proud that her partner had made such a smart decision. She then looked to Duran and said: "So you two *were* in agreement to let me go?"

"Look," Hilton said. "It would look completely foolish for us to do that right now. We realize that we can't terminate the current agreement. By this time tomorrow, the media is going to be very interested in you and you're going to probably have to fight off reporters. The fact that you came out of retirement to work and managed to bring down a serial killer makes the story even hotter. But what we *can* ask of you is that you take a break for a bit. We will not call for your assistance for several weeks. And when we do, it will likely be for something a bit more subtle."

"I'll take the blame for that," Duran said. "This case came up, there were no leads at all and I thought of you. Despite the sparse agreement we have with you, you remain one of the better agents we have."

"Thank you."

"But I must stress this," Hilton said. "In the future, any reckless disobedience or disrespect to either your director or those above him will be met with consequences. Perhaps even criminal charges. Am I understood, Agent Wise?"

"Yes sir."

Hilton nodded and got to his feet. "Now... with that out of the way..."

He extended his hand. Kate looked to Duran and only received a smile and a shrug. Kate took the offered hand and shook it.

"Damned good work, Agent Wise. You and Agent DeMarco make an incredible team."

"We really do. And I appreciate it, sir."

She paused a beat, giving them one more chance to say any last words that were on their mind. There was still tension in the air, weighed by unspoken words. After a few more seconds, Kate took her leave. She supposed there was always meant to be some sort of tension among her and Duran in this new agreement she'd signed up for. But now that Section Chief Hilton was also making himself more prominently involved, it opened up a whole new level of awareness for her.

But that was okay. She'd be fifty-six in a few weeks. How long did she really think she could keep up with this pace anyway?

She smiled as she stepped back onto the elevators, fully prepared to just get a nice hotel room somewhere in the city and sleep in tomorrow before heading back home.

How long can *I keep up with this pace?* she wondered.

Despite the soreness in her head and the memory of DeMarco taking down Insbrook as he towered above her, she was surprised to find that the answer came easily.

She'd stick with it for as long as she could.

CHAPTER TWENTY SEVEN

Kate tried to tell herself that it was silly to be so nervous about having lunch with her daughter, but the nerves remained. She checked her watch and saw that it was 12:05, an entire five minutes past the time they were supposed to meet. Kate did her best to remind herself that Melissa was perpetually late and the five minutes meant nothing.

She supposed she was so nervous because the talk she planned to have with Melissa was one she should have had years ago—probably before Melissa had been married. But Kate knew she had never been the most insightful parent. Hell, she'd put off the birds and the bees speech so long that Michael, her late husband, had ended up having it with her... and that had been only after they'd discovered Melissa had been having sex at the age of fifteen.

Sometimes it was hard to even imagine Melissa as a fifteen-year-old. It felt like looking through some dark glass at a scene on the other side. The shapes were certainly there but they were murky and far away.

It was 12:07 when Melissa finally came through the door of the little delicatessen Kate had chosen. There weren't many tables in the place, so Melissa spotted her right away and joined her. It was the first time Melissa had seen her mother since Kate had gotten back to Richmond from the Frankfield case. Spotting the bruise on the side of her mother's face, Melissa cringed.

"Some warning might have been due here," Melissa said. "Jesus, Mom, what happened?"

"What happened is that I stopped a serial killer."

"Just how serial are we talking?"

Part of her wanted to give the number—to show her daughter that the bruise on the side of her head and the shitty attitude she'd had last week had all been for a purpose. But she did not want to flaunt her success, nor did she want to make light of the twenty-three women who had lost their lives to Darby Insbrook.

"It was pretty bad," she said. "And while I know it's no excuse, it was the case that made me so distant and cold when you were trying to reach out."

"Mom...if you just wanted to have lunch to apologize..."

"No, it's more than that. It's...you know what? Let's go order our sandwiches and revisit this, okay?"

Melissa nodded, already seeming flustered. They ordered their food without speaking to one another, going through the deli line as if they were complete strangers. Even when they were back at their seats with their food, it took two or three minutes before either of them could summon the courage to speak again.

"So how'd you get the bruise?" Melissa asked.

"Because I'm fifty-five and trying to act like I'm still thirty."

Melissa touched her nose and smiled, a *that's on the nose* signal with a bit too much sass for Kate's liking. But she also knew Melissa was right.

"Believe it or not, no, I did not ask you to come here so I could apologize," Kate said. "I came here to check in on you. When I got called away on the case—"

"—and left my baby with your boyfriend," Melissa pointed out.

Kate nodded and carried on as best as she could without showing her emotion. "You told me that you and Terry were having problems. And I waved it off. At the time, I was thinking: *Yeah, well, welcome to marriage. We've all had issues.* But that's not how I should have reacted. I should have been supportive and asked questions. I should have made you a priority."

"I don't need to be your number one priority," Melissa said. "I'm not a child. But I do need to rely on you as a grandmother. You and I...we don't exactly have any extended family. And with my marriage on the ropes, you're the only other person Michelle and I can really rely on. You get that, right?"

"I do. And I love being a grandmother. It's just ... I don't know. I got the opportunity to kind of resurrect my career at the same time you were pregnant. I had these two worlds colliding and, if I'm being honest, I was selfish. Hell, I'm *still* being selfish."

"You are. And that's okay. I've said it before and I'll say it again: I love the fact that you're still an agent. And still a badass. My daughter is going to have this super-strong woman in her life and I love that."

"You're strong, too, Melissa."

"Oh, really? Look at me, Mom. Shitty job, sloppy husband ... and I run to my mommy when things get hard."

Kate knew what else she wanted to say but swallowed it back for now. Something else came to her then, something that seemed much more pressing. "This case ... I had to speak to husbands who had just lost their wives. And for the most part, they were very negligent. They did not pay their wives any attention. I think deep down, they did love their wives, but they were terrible at showing it. They were too obsessed with work and too busy providing for their wives to show them, on occasion, how much they loved them. It made me think of you and the issues you were trying to tell me about before I left for the case. And I just want so more for you than that. I started seeing you in place of those women and it ..."

She trailed off here, realizing that she was about to cry. Melissa moved her hand as if she might reach out, but she stopped herself.

"I know how important your work is," she said. "I've always known. And it's okay ..."

"I feel like I have to evolve or something," Kate said. "I'll be fifty-six soon and I still need to mature."

"What the hell are you talking about?"

"I ... Melissa, I hate to say it, but I can't solve all of your problems. Even if I wanted to, I can't. Of course, I'll always be there for you and your family. When we had the health scare two months back ... it opened my eyes to how much you and Michelle mean to me. But when it comes to everyday things … I still have a hard time with it. This whole second career thing has made me realize that I won't be around forever, even though I know I live as if I will. And if you rely too heavily on me, I fear that you might become like one of those women from the case—far too reliant on someone and not knowing what it was to be loved. Where I am in life right now, I just can't be your go-to problem solver. Does that make sense?"

"It does. And I get it. I just … I want Michelle to have a grandmother she loves and respects. And I have to know you're there for her. I have to know you care for her—and for *me*—just as much as you care for Agent DeMarco and the people you try to save on these cases."

It hurt to hear those words from Melissa's mouth, but she understood. She nodded and, carefully measuring each word, said, "I do. I love you both more than I can explain. And maybe that's why I create that distance. The things I see with work … and after your father being killed … it's almost like I'm afraid to really go deep. Even with you …"

This time the tears did come and when they did, Melissa came over to her side of the booth and placed an arm around her. "I love you, Mom."

"I know. And I love you, too. And when we're done here I think I'd like to go somewhere with you and Michelle."

"Where?"

"I don't care. Anywhere. Where would you like to go?"

"A beach. Somewhere where the surf is loud and there aren't many tourists."

"We can do that. I'll start making the plans this evening."

Melissa smiled and looked at her mother as if she had gone crazy. "Are you sure?"

"Yes."

"Great. Just … can you do one thing for me before you start planning?"

"Anything. What?"

184

"Plan your trip with Alan first. He mentioned that you guys were going away to wine country or something. A weekend getaway, right?"

"Right."

"Give him a call. If you're going to *evolve*, as you put it, I think he's part of it. And between you and me, if you keep pushing him away, I don't know how much longer he'll keep coming back. I'll always be here. But with him ... who knows?"

Kate sighed. She was fine with Melissa being right about most things, but this one ... well, this one hurt. Not only because it was true, but because it showed that Melissa was more in tune with her life than Kate realized.

It made Kate realize, with great embarrassment, that maybe her daughter was the more mature grown-up between the two of them.

The reunion with Alan went just about the way she figured it would. He took one look at the bruise on the side of her head and instantly went into caretaker mode. Even when she insisted she had been medically cleared and that the bruise was actually fading, he did not relent. After asking a barrage of questions about how it had happened and what the doctors had said, he finally eased down.

They were sitting on the couch, holding hands but with some distance between them, when Kate did her best to venture into what could be troubled waters.

"I can't tell you how much I appreciate what you did for me ... keeping Michelle while I had to leave."

"It's okay. I just need to know ... disappointing me and letting Melissa down ....was it worth it?"

"I hate to say it, but yes. I'm going to tell you something that I did not tell Melissa, so I'd appreciate it if you wouldn't tell her. This stays between the two of us, okay?"

"Sure."

She told him about the case in fine detail—about how the man she and DeMarco had brought down was responsible for twenty-three murders over the course of a little less than three years and how until they finally tracked him down, the killer had somehow gone undetected by law enforcement or the FBI.

He looked awed when she was done. He wore the expression of someone who had just finished watching an extremely thought-provoking movie. "Okay, so even I would agree that wrapping a case that resulted in the capture of such a deranged man was indeed worth leaving on such short notice. But the thing that bothers me still is that you left without knowing it would come to that. You had no idea what the case would entail or what the end of it would be."

"You're right. And it's like I told Melissa...I know I need to change that. If I'm going to finally figure out how to be a good mother and a good grandmother, I need to find that balance..."

"I can't imagine how hard it is."

"I'm sorry, Alan. I really am."

He shrugged and slid closer to her. "While we're apologizing, I think I owe you one, too. I more or less gave you an ultimatum that made it sound like I needed you to choose: me or the job. And that wasn't fair. I said it in the heat of the moment, out of anger, because we had just started planning that trip."

"Well, maybe I deserved it. And maybe we can patch it up by planning the trip again."

"I'd like that," Alan said. "But only if you're sure. I don't want to force it."

"No, I want to. And for now, the bureau has essentially told me not to expect any calls for a few months."

Alan made a show of checking over the bruise on her head and said: "You don't say. And speaking of which, I think I do have the right to ask a simple question."

"What's that?"

"How long do you plan to stick with it?"

Kate considered it for a moment, thinking of the train of thought that had gone through her head after speaking with Duran and Hilton. She did not think she was ready to hang it up just yet, but she also knew that Father Time had a way of having his say whenever he felt like it.

"For as long as I'm able to help," she answered.

"I figured you'd say that," Alan said. He then leaned in and gave her a sweet and brief kiss on the corner of her mouth. "Now let's see what we can do about still taking that trip."

"You're sure?" she asked. "I mean to echo your question … how much longer do you think you can tolerate me?"

He smiled and kissed her again before giving her previous answer right back to her.

"For as long as I'm able to help."

Now Available for Pre-Order!

IF SHE FEARED
(A Kate Wise Mystery—Book 6)

"A masterpiece of thriller and mystery. Blake Pierce did a magnificent job developing characters with a psychological side so well described that we feel inside their minds, follow their fears and cheer for their success. Full of twists, this book will keep you awake until the turn of the last page."
—Books and Movie Reviews, Roberto Mattos (re Once Gone)

IF SHE FEARED (A Kate Wise Mystery) is book #6 in a new psychological thriller series by bestselling author Blake Pierce, whose #1 bestseller Once Gone (Book #1) (a free download) has received over 1,000 five star reviews.

When another woman is found dead in a vacant, suburban house, the FBI must call in brilliant FBI special agent Kate Wise, 55, and ask her to come out of retirement from her suburban life to find the psychotic killer.

But why is the killer staging the bodies in empty houses in suburbia?

What do the victims have in common?

And can Kate, despite her age, stop him in time to save another woman's life?

An action-packed thriller with heart-pounding suspense, IF SHE FEARED is book #6 in a riveting new series that will leave you turning pages late into the night.

Book #7 in the KATE WISE MYSTERY SERIES will be available soon.

IF SHE FEARED
(A Kate Wise Mystery—Book 6)

Did you know that I've written multiple novels in the mystery genre? If you haven't read all my series, click the image below to download a series starter!

Made in the USA
Coppell, TX
10 November 2020